"There is good news and bad news here."

"Don't tell me... The good news is that I get to spend an extra few hours with you? Though, if you ask me...I'd say it could also be considered bad news as well." She looked him square in the eye, like she was measuring his response.

"If we stay put, it would be dangerous, as night temps are supposed to be brutally cold. Yet if we hike out, any number of things could go wrong. I don't want to put you in harm's way again, but I don't think it's avoidable."

The rosy color returned to her cheeks. "I've never been the kind of girl who sat around and waited to be rescued."

He'd always found that it was the women who didn't need saving were the ones he fell for the hardest... and hurt him the most when they left him in the wind.

HELICOPTER RESCUE

DANICA WINTERS

*To my readers, I appreciate your support more than you
could ever know.*

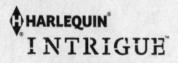

HARLEQUIN®
INTRIGUE™

Recycling programs
for this product may
not exist in your area.

ISBN-13: 978-1-335-59069-5

Helicopter Rescue

Copyright © 2024 by Danica Winters

For questions and comments about the quality of this book,
please contact us at CustomerService@Harlequin.com.

Harlequin Enterprises ULC
22 Adelaide St. West, 41st Floor
Toronto, Ontario M5H 4E3, Canada
www.Harlequin.com

Printed in U.S.A.

Danica Winters is a multiple-award-winning, bestselling author who writes books that grip readers with their ability to drive emotion through suspense and occasionally a touch of magic. When she's not working, she can be found in the wilds of Montana, testing her patience while she tries to hone her skills at various crafts—quilting, pottery and painting are not her areas of expertise. She believes the cup is neither half-full nor half-empty, but it better be filled with wine. Visit her website at danicawinters.net.

Books by Danica Winters

Harlequin Intrigue

Big Sky Search and Rescue

Helicopter Rescue

STEALTH: Shadow Team

A Loaded Question
Rescue Mission: Secret Child
A Judge's Secrets
K-9 Recovery
Lone Wolf Bounty Hunter
Montana Wilderness Pursuit

Stealth

Hidden Truth
In His Sights
Her Assassin For Hire
Protective Operation

Mystery Christmas

Ms. Calculation
Mr. Serious
Mr. Taken
Ms. Demeanor

Visit the Author Profile page at Harlequin.com.

CAST OF CHARACTERS

Kristin Loren—When someone needs help, she is the first one everyone calls. Dependable, strong and never one to pull punches, Kristin is the woman any man would be lucky to have at his side when the world comes crashing down.

Casper Keller—Casper is a former military spec ops helicopter pilot, and the name of his game is knowing when to take orders and when to give them—but his world is turned upside down when he is faced with Kristin Loren.

Hugh Keller—Casper and William's father, who is suffering from advanced Alzheimer's and goes missing in the rimrocks outside Billings, Montana.

Greg Holmes—Kristin's ex-boyfriend who is nothing more than a hotheaded jerk with an ego the size of Texas.

Michelle Keller—William's estranged wife, who sells life insurance. She loves to work, run and be outdoors. If she isn't careful, her passions may be her downfall.

William Keller—Casper's brother, who becomes a hermit after Michelle decides to leave him in charge of Hugh and his nursing duties. With everything on his shoulders, his reclusive ways nearly cost him his sanity and his life.

Chapter One

The man stepped out of the ditch, a stuffed lobster dragging on the ground behind him. The orange bailing twine was looped around the animal's neck, and the lobster bounced like it was hoping for the sweet release of a figurative death—if only it could have been so lucky. Instead, it was the perpetual stuffed clown of a man who seemed to have as much apathy toward the thing as he did self-awareness.

Kristin Loren glanced down at the man's Bermuda shorts, one leg markedly longer than the other and tattered and torn, with a strip of hibiscus-printed cloth flapping against his leg as he teetered toward them.

From what she had been told about the man, he was in his eighties, was a former dean of the physics department at CalTech and suffered from Alzheimer's. Seeing him now, his ripped and dirty clothes, and stumbling gait, she had a hard time seeing him as the powerful authority on astrophysics that, according to the internet, he had once been. He was proof of the ravaging effects of the disease, and how it could even bring an intellectual juggernaut to his knees.

Perhaps one day in the not-so-distant future, due to her own family's history of Alzheimer's, she would be found like this man had been, confused and disoriented and smelling of sweat and urine. She hoped not, but it made the ache in her chest for the man intensify.

"Wh-where am I?" the man stammered, a look of uncertainty in his eyes. "Who're you?"

"I'm Kristin. What's your name?" she asked, hoping the man was capable of answering.

"I'm Hugh." He pointed at the flight crew as the nurse approached. "Who are they?"

"We were sent out here to help you get back home. That is Greg," she said, motioning toward the pilot, "and he will be helping to make sure you make it home safely. This lady here—" she indicated the thirtysomething brunette woman at her side "—is a sweet nurse who wants to get you medical assistance. Okay?"

The nurse smiled up at Hugh. "Is it okay with you if I check your vitals really quick?"

The man frowned but nodded, then pulled the lobster into his arms like he was not an eighty-seven-year-old man and was instead a seven-year-old boy. The nurse set to work, slipping on her stethoscope.

"How are you feeling this afternoon, sir?" the nurse asked.

"I'm fine," the man said, shrugging. The man seemed not to realize they had spent nearly a day looking for him, or that the nurse appeared to be slightly alarmed by his condition.

According to his son, the man had managed to escape the confines of their home and disappeared into the night. They had only noticed he was missing when they woke up and found the man wasn't in his recliner watching reruns of *The Price is Right*.

She could almost imagine Bob Barker yelling "Come on down…" as this man with a stuffed lobster rocked away, engrossed. Then again, at the thought, she could understand why the man would have wanted to get up, slip out and disappear into the scrubby landscape of the rimrocks.

"You look nice," the man said to Kristin, seeming to forget about the nurse as she worked. A droopy, sad smile adorned his lips like forgotten party streamers left to the rain.

"Well, thank you. You look nice yourself." She sent him the closest thing to a real smile as she could muster. He deserved some respite from the chaos in his mind, if even just for a moment, thanks to her fleeting grin.

Kristin had been on so many of these types of calls for search-and-rescue that most didn't really faze her anymore, but there was something about this old-timer that pulled at her. Perhaps it was his utter lack of understanding, or the way he had seemed to look into her soul when he spoke. He reminded her of her grandfather in the last years of his life, when she was small enough to pull on his beard and whisper Popsicle-stick jokes into his failing ears.

She missed him.

"Do you remember your full name, Hugh?" she asked, glancing over her shoulder at the double-bladed helo that rested in the pasture behind her.

The man's gaze slipped toward the helicopter. "I used to fly in the war," he said, not bothering to acknowledge, or not knowing the answer to, her question.

She'd long ago learned that the best way to get answers from someone who was aggressive or confused was to take a round-about approach. The wrong style of communication in fragile situations only led to undesirable results. For now, it was imperative that she handle him gently so that they could get him into the helicopter and transport him to the hospital in Billings, and hopefully then get back into the hands of his family.

"Which war were you involved in?" Kristin asked.

He stumbled as he took a step and she put his arm around her shoulder, helping him to walk. "Vietnam. Did two tours." He glanced up at the sky, then covered his eyes as if he was staring into the midday sun. "I should have never made it out."

She wasn't sure if that was a statement or a wish; either way, the agony of his tone set against the precariousness of his situation made her want to sob, but she couldn't pay heed to her emotions when there was a life to be saved.

"His BP is pretty low. We need to get him some fluids and get him stabilized so the doctors can sort him out," the nurse said as she moved to the other side and helped to walk him toward the helicopter as Kristin tried to keep chatting with the somewhat listless man.

By keeping him talking about the details of his war years, it didn't take long to get him loaded. They spent the next forty-five minutes pushing IV fluids while she and Hugh chatted about her job at FLIR Tech and their forward-looking infrared equipment that they had used to locate him in the field near the edge of a sage-lined cliff. Every time she tried to get him to answer more questions about his identity or where he lived, he avoided them and turned the conversation back to his younger years.

She watched as the nurse on the flight took the man's blood pressure as they neared the helo pad outside the hospital. The nurse's face pinched, and she took it again.

"Everything okay?"

The nurse seemed not to hear her, and instead glanced over at the EKG monitor. The green lines on the screen were jagged and irregular, like the thrusting peaks and valleys of freshly shorn mountains. Kristin didn't know a great deal about the line on the screen, but she knew enough to realize that with a heart rate at 43 bpm and a read like what she was seeing, it didn't point at anything good.

The nurse took out a syringe, then glanced down at her watch and turned to the pilot. "How much longer until we touch down?"

The pilot pointed down at the ground, where Kristin could just make out the red circle with an *H* in its center. As they got closer, she saw a group of personnel waiting near the doors of the hospital with a gurney.

Reaching down, Kristin took Hugh's hand. He looked up at her, his actions slow and deliberate, as though he was struggling to control his body. "It's going to be okay, Hugh," she said, positioning the lobster deeper into the nook of his arm. "We're at the hospital. They're going to take you from here and get you the help you need."

He answered her with a broken nod and an almost imperceptible squeeze of her fingers. The chill of his skin made her wonder if this simple exchange would be one of his last.

"Tell my son…" He took in a gasping breath as the nurse plunged the needle into his arm. "Tell him, I'm sorry."

The man closed his eyes just as the helicopter touched down. Before the blades even stopped rotating, there was a rush of nurses and hospital staff, and Kristin was pushed out of the way. Hugh was pulled onto the pad and put on the gurney, then he was whisked out of sight, into the belly of the industrial building.

She wanted to follow him, to make sure that he would be okay and that she had been wrong in her thoughts. The man hadn't been hurt, only left in the elements for too long. He couldn't be dying…not on her watch. If anything, she had just let her fears get the better of her. There had been dozens of other rescues she had taken part in where the persons they had rescued were in far more precarious medical states and had pulled through.

Hugh would be fine.

Yet, she couldn't help but step out of the helo

and make her way inside the hospital in hopes of hearing good news. The staff had disappeared into the triage area, so Kristin made her way to the waiting area. It was empty, aside from a couple holding a small, ruddy-cheeked baby who was pulling at his ear and starting to cry. The poor mother had dark circles under her eyes and the father was pacing, as if each step would bring them closer to relief for their child.

She wasn't a parent, but there was no amount of pacing that could quell another's pain—she was well-acquainted with that concept.

After ten minutes or so, she was unable to watch any more of the parents' struggle and she made her way to the check-in area. "I'm part of the flight crew that came in with Hugh Keller. I was wondering if you have an update on his status?"

The secretary behind the desk nodded, the action stoic. "Hold on for just a moment and let me check for you."

As the secretary headed for the glass doors leading to the ER, the automatic doors at the entranceway slid open and a man came rushing in from outside. He was wearing blue-tinted Costa sunglasses and a tight-fitting, gray V-necked shirt that accentuated all the muscular curves and bumps of his body. Though she couldn't explain why, she caught herself catching her breath as she stared at him. He definitely wasn't bad-looking; in fact, she could safely say he was the hottest man she had seen in person in a long time. But standing here and waiting on a man's medical status seemed like the last moment that she should have found herself stunned by a handsome brunette.

The man walked up beside her and she caught a whiff of expensive cologne, made stronger by his body heat. If she had to guess, it was Yves Saint Laurent or some other haute scent, but as quickly as she tried to name it, she noted how out of place it was in the industrial austerity of where they were standing.

"Is there anyone working here?" he grumbled, tapping on the counter.

"She just ran to check on something for me. I'm sure she will be back in a sec," she said, her initial attraction somewhat dampened by the man's annoyance.

The man grumbled something unintelligible under his breath, but she was sure it was a string of masked expletives and she frowned.

"Sorry," the guy said, finally seeming to notice that she was a real live person and not just a source of information. "I'm not trying to be an ass... It's just..." He ran his hands over his face and bumped against his sunglasses, realizing he still had them on. He gave a dry chuckle as he took them off, then looked up at her with eyes that were even more blue than the lenses on his glasses. She thought he was handsome before, but now he was absolutely stunning and she found herself unable to look away. "It's been a long day."

"Uh-huh. I get it." She glanced at the little line next to his mouth, a crease that came from a life of smiling—which seemed at odds with his current mood.

"My father. Yeah…" He paused. "They recently brought him in."

Just like that, she was whipped back to reality. She couldn't just ask who he was because of privacy laws, but even without knowing his father's name, she could tell from the shape of his eyes and the curve of his nose that he was Hugh's son. She wasn't sure how she could have missed it until now. There was no denying that the man before her was a younger version of the man whom she had found deep in the middle of nowhere.

"I'm sure your father is going to be okay."

His face darkened, but she wasn't sure if it was because he feared that it was an empty platitude, or if he was actually angry at her for her attempt to mollify him—either way, she wanted to make that look disappear.

The glass door through which the secretary

had disappeared reopened and she walked out. She glanced over at the man at Kristin's side, then back to her. The woman raised her eyebrows, a silent question. Kristin gave her a furtive nod.

"The man you accompanied, Hugh, is currently with the doctor."

"Hugh? Hugh Keller?" the man asked.

The secretary nodded.

The man gripped the edge of the counter. "That's my father. I'm Casper Keller. I'm going to need more information. What's the doctor saying? Is he going to be all right?"

The secretary's mouth opened and closed, as if she was hoping the right words would just magically appear on her lips in this challenging situation. "I… I'm afraid I can't speak to—"

"But you have an answer. Please, if this was your father…" Casper pleaded, making Kristin's chest ache. "Please."

The secretary wrung her hands and looked down at the desk. "I'm sorry, Mr. Keller." There was an agonizing pause before the woman finally looked up. There were tears in her eyes. "I heard the doctor say he didn't think your father will survive. I'll try and get you back to see him." The secretary turned and slipped back through the door.

Kristin didn't know what to do to comfort

the man when her heart was breaking for both
Casper and the man who had reminded her so
much of her grandfather. Something about this
situation made it feel like she was losing the
patriarch of her family again.

"I'm so sorry, Casper."

He looked at her, but there was no recogni-
tion in his eyes, and the look was so much like
his father's that she was thrown off balance.
"Yeah."

In that single, breathless word, she felt every
ounce of his loss...and it tore her to pieces.

Chapter Two

The incident command trailer was parked to the left of the pad as Casper set down the helicopter beside an AgustaWestland AW101 helo that was geared up to the hilt—it even had a large ball-shaped camera unit on the nose. He couldn't wait to get back to work after losing his father a couple of weeks ago. He would never understand how his father had gone missing so far from his brother's place, but there was no going back and righting wrongs—there was only accepting that their father was dead.

The second his phone picked up reception, thanks to the myriad of communication networks the tech gurus had set up at their base camp, he was flooded with a wave of notifications.

Speak of the devil. Of course, his brother, William, had texted.

He opened up the three messages his brother had sent. The first was a long and rambling diatribe of what could best be described as him seeking absolution. From the time stamp, it appeared as though William had sent that one in the middle of the night, probably between glasses three and four of whiskey.

Casper didn't want to admit to himself that he found a certain amount of comfort in his brother's downward spiral of guilt—William had it coming. Yet, in the same thought, he didn't wish it for him. William and his wife, Michelle, had stepped up to the plate in a way he never could have...and, truthfully, he wasn't sure that he could have emotionally handled. Before this mishap, he had been singing their praises, so to go in direct opposition and criticize their generosity now only made him feel like the worst kind of person.

Regardless, his brother could wait for him to text back.

Work. I just need to work.

Casper unstrapped himself and got out of the bird, making his way onto the pad. It felt good to stand up and walk, after flying for the last hour in near darkness and questionable winds. Truth be told, though, he loved flying in the kinds of conditions that would make lesser men's asses pucker. It was as if each time, he proved his merit not only as a good pilot, but also as a better man.

Many could fly like he could, but what he prided himself upon—and what he hoped put him above many others in his line of work—was his integrity and honor. These qualities had been hammered into him during his time as a pilot in the army, and they would be his core values until the day he died.

It was just too bad he couldn't say the same of his brother, setting aside his caretaking…though even that could now be called into question.

Damn it. I can't go there. It doesn't do a damn bit of good.

He unzipped his flight jacket, taking in the cool summer morning as he gave one more look at the horizon. The sun was finally starting to climb over the tops of the mountains, reminding him of the scale of the things going on in his life. The pain he was feeling, and the anger, wouldn't last forever—nothing did.

The flaps at the front of the canvas-wall tent were tied back and he made his way into the base camp's incident command center. It was abuzz with people talking. At first glance, there had to be about fifteen people standing around, mostly men. The SAR team leader, Cindy, spotted him and gave a quick wave, and he made his way over to her and the group of people she was standing with.

He recognized most of the people in the room

as fellow SAR members, but there was also a smattering of new faces. They had just done a recruitment and this was the first training event with the new people. He couldn't say he was overly thrilled, but it was nice to get some fresh blood. They needed a shake-up to bring in updated ideas and methods, even if it was a bit like teaching old dogs new tricks.

Cindy gave him her trademark strained-lip smile, the one that made him wonder if it actually hurt. "Glad to see you made it. You ready for this fun?"

"About as ready as a dog is to go to the vet." He smirked.

Cindy chuckled. "Why do I get the sense that you'd be far more at home in a vet's office than a doctor's?"

"Hey, now, you calling me a dog?" His grin widened.

"If the shoe fits," she said with a laugh. "You know I heard about you and your pack of girl-friends."

He laughed and it felt out of place—he was riddled with guilt. At a time like this, having just lost his dad, what right did he have to joke around?

She must have sensed that her comment had struck a nerve. "By the way, Casper, I'm real sorry to hear about your old man. It's always tough losing a parent."

"I appreciate that," he said in a clipped tone. "How many newbies do we have on our hands this round?" he asked, moving his chin in the direction of four new faces.

"We have six coming in—we're going to break them in or break them down." Cindy put her hand on his shoulder, letting their real conversation pass by with as much sentiment as either could muster. "By the way, I have you training with a FLIR Tech employee today. She's supposed to be the best of the best in this new and burgeoning technology. Be warned, I was told she has a bit of a chip on her shoulder."

"Great. Can't wait to see what that means."

"Oh, I can tell you exactly what it means—she is going to be a pain in your ass." Cindy paused, looking in the direction of the tent's entrance. "Actually, it looks like she is ready to start chapping you right about now."

He turned in the direction of Cindy's gaze and walking in was none other than the stunning, yet beguiling, blond woman he had first talked to at the hospital ER in Billings. The woman stopped and stared at him, as though she was just as surprised to see him. She stumbled as she recognized him, but then regained her composure, drew back her shoulders and moved toward them. However, from the pace of her tentative steps, he could sense she was hesitant to speak to him.

As she neared, Cindy began, "This is Kristin Loren, your newest—"

"Oh, we've met before," he said, cutting off Cindy. "What're you doing here?" He hadn't meant to come off as brusque, but there was no taking back his near growl.

She took a step back from him as if she was moving away from a punch square to the gut. "I'm here as an instructor—teaching one of the tracks on using tech in rescue situations…like your father's."

He flashed back to the first time he had seen her. She had been wearing jeans and a sweatshirt, nothing that would have given away her identity as the woman who had likely held a pivotal role in getting his dad to the hospital in time for him to receive care.

Just like that, he found himself the heel.

If it wasn't for Kristin, his father would have likely never been found…or rather, found alive. His father had died in comfort and peace, instead of lost in the woods, confused and wandering. He owed her his thanks, not his derision.

"Kristin, I'm—"

She gave him a warm smile that told him he was forgiven, but it didn't assuage his guilt.

"I'm truly sorry for your loss," she said.

"Thank you and I apologize for being…less than welcoming." He offered her his hand and she graciously accepted the meager apology. "It's why Cindy, here—" he let go and motioned toward the SAR leader "—doesn't usually let me be the public face of the organization. Smart move on her part, really. I do best in the sky."

"You're the eyes in the sky for the whole crew. I would say that you are a critical part of our group," Cindy said, giving him a quick blow to the shoulder. "You're not going to be getting any other compliments, so you better write that one down."

Casper rubbed where she had struck him, feigning pain as he laughed. "I'm surprised you even assume I can write, the way you talk about me most of the time," he teased.

"You're not wrong," Cindy countered, smiling. "Which brings me back to why we are here—I am hoping you and Kristin can get along. Nonetheless, she has graciously agreed to put up with you for the next few days."

"Great. What're we going to be working on?" he asked, smiling at Kristin.

"FLIR. And *speaking of* you being the hapless face of our organization, unwitting or not, we need you to get us some good press about the FLIR program so we can get public funding to get our own equipment." Cindy gave him a serious expression.

He hated playing politics, but in the world of search-and-rescue, it was critical. The community held the figurative purse strings and it was make-or-break that they kept a positive reputation in the court of public opinion. Nothing was better than making timely rescues, rather than recovering remains. It was also critical for their team's morale that they saved lives. Bringing loved ones home to their families was what kept many of them going in their intense and brutal calling.

"That your bird out there on the pad?"

Kristin nodded. "My team's pilot is over there," she said, motioning to a thin-shouldered guy with a receding hairline.

"Oh…" he said, the sting to his ego echoing in his voice. He glanced at Cindy. "I guess I'll be riding shotgun."

Cindy laughed. "Only if you're not up to flying the beast."

Kristin gave a slight nod. "You know how to fly her?"

He couldn't control the smile that overtook his face. "I can fly anything with a rotor."

Cindy nodded her approval, but there was concern in her eyes. "Just make sure that you grab your information packet, get yourself up to speed on the training scenario and then bring her back in one piece—we can't afford to replace it and we certainly can't afford to have you doing something stupid."

"You can trust me. I'd never let you or the team down." As he spoke, he could feel the weight of his words press down on him.

"I have no doubts," Cindy said, turning to Kristin. "You need to make sure you keep an eye on him, though. Casper is a top-notch pilot, but a lot is riding on this flight."

"As long as he listens to my instruction, we should be all good." Kristin smiled, and as he looked into her green eyes, he wondered if his role with SAR wasn't the only thing on the line.

Chapter Three

Casper opened up the throttle and he went light on the skids. The red-and-yellow SAR trailer parked near the pad pitched from the pressure of the rotor wash. Casper neutralized the helicopter's movements and readied to lift. He loved that feeling—the moment of calm right before the storm.

He was excited to show her what he could do on the sticks, while also getting the job done and learning about her work. He glanced over at Kristin for one last preflight check. Her blond braid was poking out over the collar of her coat, beneath her flight helmet. Her expression was tense, as if their flight relied on the strength of her concentration and willpower, and not his flying abilities. As if she could feel his gaze upon her, she sent him a sidelong glance, but he wasn't sure if the look in her eyes was one of excitement or concern. If anything, the slight squint of her eyes only made her more interest-ing—a mystery that was waiting to be solved.

"My team has set up a small, smokeless fire for us to find a hypothetical missing hiker. The current search radius is based on the hiker hav-ing a two-day head start from the PLS. Often, as I'm sure you know, when people go missing, they are told to build a fire and stay put. This way, we can train in typical conditions. Okay?" She sounded a bit nervous.

"Two days from point last seen. Roger."

According to Cindy, Kristin had spent thou-sands of hours working with FLIR cameras, sensors and the accompanying tech, which had to have meant she had nearly as many hours as him in the belly of a helo. Yet, in watching her, he wasn't sure his assumptions had been on point.

"Ready to rock and roll?" Casper gave her a thin smile and a thumbs-up.

She answered with a nod almost as stiff as her back. "You going to lift off or stare at me all day?" she said, sending him a mischievous grin.

Maybe there really was hope for a working friendship between them.

"I wasn't staring at you. Don't get ahead of yourself there, dude." He smirked, loving the way her eyes squinted with the hard jab to the friend zone.

She laughed, but there was a touch of mirth in the sound. "You know, between the two of us, you are the more replaceable on this assignment. Watch yourself."

There was a certain sting in her words that made him wonder if he had taken his teasing a step too far. He was probably just imagining things and she was merely fighting fire with fire. Regardless, it made him like her incrementally more, and at the same time, want to pull pitch and press her back in her seat so hard that she would question the nature of life.

He lifted the skids off the ground and they took to the sky. According to Kristin's training module, the fake missing hikers were within a fifteen-mile radius of their PLS, a pin on a map sent to them by Cindy.

In real rescues, one of their major battles was against the weather—both for their teams and for the people they were tasked with locating. In the winter, the wind chill and the snow-pack could greatly hamper any rescue attempts. Often, the victims would attempt to build a fire, but the fires tended to be small because of the lack of dry wood. In those cases, FLIR would definitely give them an edge in spotting the minuscule heat source and getting their teams to the exact location of missing persons instead of spending valuable limited time in trying to locate.

Seconds in a search often became the thin line between life and death. There were none to waste.

He always liked training missions where he got to show his true colors. It was a nice break from the civil flight crew he had joined after leaving the army. In his former line of work, before he'd retired as a chief warrant officer and Black Hawk pilot for the 160th SOAR, he'd had the chance to do this kind of thing about as often as he wanted to, and was always honing his skills. Since then, he could feel himself rusting. He hated the eroding sensation.

He looked out at the pitted, shadowy summits of Lone Mountain and Wilson Peak, which protected Big Sky. They reminded him of his last active mission, when he had attempted to rescue two SEALs who had found themselves stranded at the top of a mountain in Northern Colorado. There were several reasons the 160th's motto was Death Waits in the Dark, but in the case of the SEALs, it had been the brutal, piercing blades of cold that had ushered them to the grave.

As they moved steadily through the sky, Kristin turned to her computer screen. The images that filled it were black-and-white, but were as crisp as if they were looking at their launch pad at the height of the day. When he'd began flying, almost twenty years ago, he'd started with little more than a tiny screen with grainy imagery. Now they could identify the heat signature of a rat denned ten feet down. It was crazy to think where the technology would be in another twenty years.

Ten minutes into the flight, he glanced over and noticed a herd of elk standing at the edge of a timberline in the FLIR images. The herd was all cows, not surprising, given the time of the year and the pressing calving season. If they hadn't been working, he would have been tempted to get closer to the herd to get a better look, but then he wasn't sure it would have made a difference given the limited light.

"How many head?" he asked.

"There has to be thirty or so, more bunched in the tree line. Hard to count."

He glanced back at the screen one more time before turning back to his duties. "Any sign of our fire?"

"Negative. We close to the PLS?"

"Five miles out, but we will be there in a few minutes." The rest of the SAR team was lined up to hike in to the same target for training, but they wouldn't be there for at least a few hours.

"Does our fake victim have any known medical conditions?"

They had gone over all the information before they had taken to the air, but Kristin mustn't have been paying attention. It annoyed him slightly, but he reminded himself that she was probably feeling about as awkward with him as he was with her.

Kristin looked over at him, but there was a tightness to her features that made him wonder if she was thinking about her last mission as well—the rescue of his father.

"No known issues."

She nodded, like her question hadn't really been to gain information, but had been to test him. If she thought she was going to catch him ill-prepared, or not up to the task, she would have another think coming.

He had been volunteering for SAR for the last few years and always focused on the task at hand—even now, with this incredibly beautiful woman by his side. Sure, he would have liked to stare at her and showboat in this borrowed bird, just to show her that she was flying with a man who had spent his life perfecting his skills...until lately.

His elbow popped as he moved the control stick, reminding him that even his body was eroding. His clock was ticking for being a good pilot and if this flight didn't go right, his position with SAR could be in jeopardy.

Even if his body and his reputation held, sometimes he worried about his soul. His last call for SAR had been an especially brutal one. A fly fisherman from Massachusetts had gotten his raft trapped in a strainer—or logjam—on the river and found himself trapped under the vessel, and deeply entrenched between a variety of snags.

He had been underwater for three days before his remains could be safely recovered. When they picked him out of the debris, he was cut up and his skin had started sloughing from his exposed hands. Fast water played havoc on remains.

He would also never forget the call when he had arrived first on scene at a small airline crash. The little commuter plane had taken a nosedive straight into the ground so hard that the pilot's body had been severed by the restraints meant to hold the man in place. The lines where the straps had moved through the body were cut with surgeon-like precision and blood had been everywhere. That one, that scene, still haunted him at night.

As if merely thinking about an airline crash could bring down their helo, he felt a sudden surge coming from the engine. He glanced at the gauges, but there was nothing that looked abnormal. Perhaps he had merely had some kind of psychosomatic response to the memory of the horribly disfigured pilot.

"You okay over there?" Kristin asked. "You look a little pale."

"Fine… Everything's fine," he said, not sure if he was being entirely honest with her.

"I wasn't asking if everything was fine," she said, leery. Her gaze moved to the instrument panel, which made him wonder if she, too, had felt the disturbance. He wasn't about to ask her if she wasn't volunteering the information.

"I'm okay," he said, faking a smile.

"Good, we are just coming over the PLS."

He looked down through the glass floor of the nose. There were no light sources from fires, flashlights or glow sticks. "You see a heat signature?"

She shook her head.

The helicopter shuddered and there was a high-pitched moaning sound. *Hydraulics.*

The damn hydraulics had failed.

He stopped moving for a moment, feeling the helicopter's power start to fade in his hands. From here on out, he would have to control this beast on straight muscle.

Goddamn it. The engines are going.

He had been through one autorotation scenario in a helicopter before, and no matter how anyone looked at it, it was nothing more than a controlled crash. If he screwed this up, they were going to die.

"Engine failed," he said, trying to sound calm and collected, though his mind was going over how their bodies would be found—usually there was a fire and very little was left. "We're going down."

He was met with dead silence from Kristin.

They were at 500 feet AGL, nose into the wind. He looked out—ahead of them was a small opening in the timber. It wasn't big, but it would have to do if there would be any chance of them making it out of this engine failure alive.

He adjusted the pitch of the blade to neutral as the rotor decayed. The upward flow of air continued to turn the disc. He lowered the collective. They started to descend as he watched his air speed and altitude, making sure everything was clear for the glide to the ground.

Arresting the descent, he pitched up and he flared. He leveled off the flight path, attempting to become parallel to the ground in an effort to reduce the forward air speed and be at the lowest rate of descent as possible. He didn't want the bird to roll when they hit.

He'd done his fair share of flying in the bush,

but there was a big difference between landing in a predetermined location and being forced to land in an autorotation situation. As they lowered, the pines enveloped them. The sweat beaded on his lip.

One limb or one downed log in the wrong spot and the bird would roll and they would both be dead.

He took a look at the ground, praying that the area was clear beneath. Near the center of the landing area was a scattering of downed timber that looked like some kind of giant game of pick-up sticks. They were going down, and damn it if they weren't screwed.

Chapter Four

On a handful of her search-and-rescue calls, Kristin had had individuals tell her they knew they were going to die. After some research, she had come to learn that moment of awareness was called terminal lucidity. According to what she'd read, it could happen moments to weeks ahead of a person's actual death. It was one hell of a phenomenon and now that she was staring at the grim reaper's scythe, she wondered when that moment would come for her.

They were falling.

At the nose of the helo, she could make out an opening in the timber—it was the only area where they had any chance of bringing down the bird without crashing directly into the huge lodgepole and ponderosa pines.

The acrid scent of hydraulic fluid permeated the air.

It had crossed her mind on more than a few of her flights that going down was a real possibility, but she had found comfort in the human condition of "it won't happen to me." Oh, how the Fates were laughing at her right now.

This isn't it. This isn't the way I'm meant to die.

She grabbed her flight harness as the bird started to descend rapidly.

As long as they could land flat and manage not to roll, they would be okay.

She thought of the helicopter crash she had been called out to three years ago. From the follow-up NTSB accident report, they had gone into an autorotation just like what she was experiencing now; except, when that crew had hit the ground, the nose had dipped and the front of the skid had struck hard and thrown them, rotor first, into the dirt. The blades had sheered and the shrapnel and the ensuing fire had taken the pilot's and passenger's lives.

A ball of fire...

Her entire body tightened.

The opening widened as they lowered. Below them was a smattering of logs. To the right, in front of them was a tiny opening; if they landed there, they had a chance of survival. Yet, at the speed and angle of their descent, there was no way they were going to make it that far. If they hit the downed timber, they were going to be just like the pilot and passenger whose bodies she had been sent in to recover.

Death happens to us all.

She watched as the timber below her grew larger.

"It's okay. You've got this," she said, glancing over at Casper.

His expression was stone-cold and deadly serious as he held the sticks and stared ahead. She wasn't sure whether or not he had heard her, but it didn't matter, as she was trying to comfort herself just as much as she was trying to comfort him.

Casper. Hell, it was like he was even named after a ghost, like even his name was an omen of the death that awaited her. Why hadn't she thought about that before?

Even if she had seen his name as some kind of macabre sign, she couldn't say that she wouldn't have gotten in this bird. Maybe it was that attitude and failure to acknowledge and respect her intuition that had gotten her here in her life. Though, if she had been frightened off of everything and anything that made her slightly uncomfortable, she would never have lived the life she had; she had done some great things— loved and lost, achieved and failed, and hoped. Above all, it had always been hoping that had gotten her through every downfall.

She looked over at Casper. There was a bead of sweat moving down his temple, like his body was preemptively crying for their loss. Casper glanced over at her, finally breaking away from his steady concentration. He gave a stiff nod, like he had finally registered what she had said and agreed they were going to be okay... Or maybe the nod was to say he was sorry, that he knew they were going down and he was to blame.

His blue eyes were dark and stormy as he turned away.

If she was going to die, at least she was going down with the most handsome man she had ever met. For these few seconds, she could be comforted by the knowledge that she might share some infinite and eternal moment with this man. It was odd, but she loved the thought and her hands loosened slightly on her harness.

Yes, relax. She exhaled as she found a tiny respite from her terror.

It was always the ones who were asleep or drunk who survived accidents—those whose bodies were completely at ease.

She had to trust Casper. He would land this. They would be safe.

Letting out a long exhale, she closed her eyes and tried to calm her body.

The bird hit hard.

The impact ran up her legs and through her spine, rattling her like she had just rear-ended a car at thirty-five. She braced herself for the pitch forward, for the impact of the roll. Yet, nothing came. No pitch. No roll.

The chopping sound of the blades overhead slowed and quieted, and the alarm pierced the air. Until now, she had barely registered the blaring sound. Now, together with those wails and the timpani drumming of her heart, her world sounded like an out-of-tune marching band.

"Are you okay?" Casper reached over and touched her arm.

His sudden touch drew open her eyes. There, feet from the glass nose of the helo, was a copse of timber. They were so close to the trees that she wasn't even sure how their blades weren't weed-whacking them down.

"Holy…" She said the word on an exhale, making it sound like a whispering wind rather than a reprieve from terror. It was as if all of her emotions filled the air of her lungs and escaped from her in one single sound.

It was strange how a whisper could hold far more power and pain than a scream.

Chapter Five

Given their situation, Kristin had taken this disaster as well as he could have hoped. She was sitting on a downed log about fifty yards from the flightless bird and tapping away on her satellite phone. By now, everyone in the training unit had to have known what had happened, and how he had not only let her down, but also his entire team.

Cindy was going to be pissed.

Casper walked around to the front of the skids. Everything looked as it should, without any bending or warping, which, given the fact they had come down hard, was impressive. The components of the bird were manufactured to take hits like that on occasion, but by the same token, hydraulic lines weren't supposed to fail in midflight, either.

The worst part of all was that he had no one to blame but himself. Though others may have pointed the finger at the last PIC, his role as the new pilot was to do a full-system check before ever leaving the ground. He had failed more than his machine had. He should have known of a potential problem.

There was a long, jagged tear in the red body of the helo where a branch from the downed log to his left had penetrated the aircraft's skin. It was incredible that the skeletal grasp of the dead tree hadn't pulled them sideways. They were damn lucky.

His gaze moved toward Kristin, who was holding the phone in her hands but was staring out at the timber around them. A gust of wind whipped up her hair, lifted it and pressed it against her wet lips. She didn't seem to notice.

It was hardly an imperfection—her hair being stuck—but the violation of her tender skin made him want to come close to her and pull it away. How could he have been jealous of a wayward lock?

He shook his head, trying to clear his mind, but found himself drawn back to the woman who had nearly been killed. The color had returned to her features and he couldn't help but see exactly how beautiful she was. Perhaps it was that she seemed at home out here in the woods, even considering what had happened.

Maybe she was like him, could find comfort in the middle of chaos more than in any moment of peace and tranquility. Even as a kid, when he had been living the latchkey lifestyle with his brother, William, the times when things seemed to be "normal" were when everything was falling apart. They had always been moving around thanks to his father's position in the army.

It had been a wonder that their mother hadn't left him outside a firehouse. She'd often talked about how, as a baby, he had never slept and had preferred to cry anytime the house was quiet. That was one reason he was a little weak in the knees whenever he thought about having a family—karma would definitely come around to bite him given half an opportunity.

"What are you looking at?" Kristin asked, breaking his stream of consciousness and pulling him back to the fact that she had probably just caught him staring.

"Sorry—" he motioned toward her mouth as he moved to her side "—you have something on your lip."

She frowned and picked the hair away.

Before she had a chance to ask him why such an inconsequential thing had managed to draw his attention, and he'd have to admit that he thought she was, hands down, the most beautiful woman he had ever seen in real life, he spoke up. "Did you manage to get ahold of your team back at the base?"

Her gaze flickered to the phone in her hands before returning to him. "This thing is slower than your reaction up there."

He stopped moving, unsure if she was condemning him for his failings or teasing him. He yearned for it to be the latter, but if he was right and she was gunning for him, he wasn't sure if he was ready to face the firing squad.

"You don't know how sorry I am." He looked down at his hands. His fingers were caked with hydraulic fluid and dust, and his fingernails were dirty. She was an adventurous woman, or so he could assume by the fact she was a SAR volunteer, just like him, but that didn't mean she would want a man like him—a grubby failure.

"I have no doubt you are sorry," she said. Her voice had taken on a soft edge that seemed to go against the directness of her statement—or was it an accusation? "Are you actively trying to kill me? If you are, tell me now and I will leave you alone."

"I wouldn't have taken her up…or you…" He reached out to touch her shoulder, but stopped, as if grazing her skin would be only further reminder of how much he could have just cost them both.

"Just don't try to kill me again. I like breathing," she said, taking his hand and pressing it gently to her shoulder as she looked up at him.

Her hand rested on his—her skin was icy and it worried him.

"I'd never want to have anyone in my care get hurt. I wouldn't—"

She waved him off. "Don't worry, I'm kidding." She squeezed his hand and then let go. "I guess I'm just really bad in these kinds of situations."

"You mean knowing how to react after you nearly lost your life?"

"Now who is the one being over-the-top?" She smiled up at him and the giant knot he hadn't known was in his chest finally loosened. "You landed that thing like you had crashed a thousand times… You *haven't*, though, have you?" She eyed him playfully.

The rest of the knot disappeared. "Yeah, that's me… The number-one crash dummy in the air today." He grunted and moved around in his best imitation of a great ape.

She giggled, covering her mouth, and the phone antenna jabbed her hard in the cheek, just below the eye. "Oh, my God," she said, dropping the phone in her lap and touching the spot beneath her eye that was already turning into a welt.

He laughed, hard. "I thought I was the accident-prone one today."

"Have you ever had one of those days—*heck,*

one of those *years*—that you just wanted to start over? Like, pretend it never happened, erase it, or whatever?"

He loved that she had actually said *whatever*. He was definitely with *his people*—not that he'd ever accidentally poked himself in the eye.

"I've had decades that I wish had never happened, but even as crappy as today has gone… I can't say that I'd want to take it back." He smiled at her.

She let go of his hand and moved slightly, and he let his fingers fall away from her jacket.

"Are you okay?" he asked.

She gave him a sidelong look, as though she wasn't sure if he was asking about her in the moment or overall.

"I mean—" he nudged his chin in the direction of the helo "—you didn't get hurt or anything, did you?" He wasn't sure he could face himself in the mirror if she was.

"I'm fine."

"That is the female equivalent of saying that you may have an arm coming out at the socket. Do I need to give you a look to assess you for damages?" He laughed, sending her a smirk that had worked on a few women in the past.

"Don't you dare look at me like that," she said, but there was a distinct ruddiness to her cheeks as she looked away from him.

There was a warmth to his cheeks as he realized how his comment had come off, and how, though she had been coquettish, he may have taken things a bit too far. "Did you hear back from base?"

She shook her head. "They haven't texted back yet—not anyone. I think my messages are sending, but these damned GPS messengers aren't known for their speed in sending and receiving texts."

That was a concept—Montana backcountry being at the hind end of the technological bandwidth—he knew all too well. There were a number of meetings he had been forced to take in the Super 1 grocery-store parking lot because it was the only place with enough speed to conduct a proper group video chat. Any more than a couple of people on Zoom and he was just about better off sending smoke signals.

Yet, that lack of tech had rarely bothered him. It was a quaint reminder he was residing in a place that put more of an emphasis on living in the moment instead of focusing on the virtual menagerie of staged social-media poses and fraudulent family photos. Montana living was gritty and ugly, a visceral reminder of nature's unforgiving bite. At the same time, the challenge and exacting manner was what made this lifestyle beautiful. The Montana wilderness was his home, through and through, and it was a place he would never leave.

"Well, there is good news and bad news here."

"Don't tell me… The good news is that I get to spend an extra few hours with you? Though, if you ask me… I'd say it could also be considered bad news as well." She looked him square in the eye, like she was measuring his response.

"I was going to say that the good and bad news is that we were going to have to start hiking out of here or stay put and wait for the team to come in and get us. If we stay put, it would be dangerous, as night temps are supposed to be brutally cold. Yet, if we hike out, any number of things could go wrong. I don't want to put you in harm's way again, but I don't think it's avoidable."

The rosy color returned to her cheeks. She rubbed at her neck and set the sat phone on the log. She chipped off a piece of wayward bark and crumbled it between her fingertips. "I've never been the kind of girl who sat around and waited to be rescued."

He'd always found that it was the women who didn't need saving who were the ones he fell for the hardest…and hurt him the most when they left him in the wind. He couldn't fall for another of that type again…no matter how sexy she was, or how hard he found himself once again staring at her lips. Why did he have to be like this? Why couldn't he be more of a *normal* dude, who could hit it and quit it when it came to the women in his life?

Then again, dudes who hit it and quit it weren't the kinds of guys he found himself hanging out with. In fact, his best friend, Leo—also a SAR member—was a hopeless romantic. So much so that he hadn't given up on the self-proclaimed love of his life, who had left him shortly after they had graduated from college. That guy was a lost cause when it came to love. At least he, Casper, wasn't that pathetic. He could get over loss... Well, at least he could *eventually*.

His last girlfriend had left him for a woman she had met on an online dating app—one swipe and everything he had built his world upon had been erased and replaced. If only his heart could have been repaired as quickly as it had been broken; and yet, he still found himself occasionally thinking about her and hoping she was doing well. Who did that after having been broken up with like he had been?

In every other respect, besides women, he would have considered himself an alpha, but damn it if the right woman couldn't do a number on him.

Yep, he definitely couldn't find himself falling again. Not until he stopped thinking about his ex, Felicia, once and for all. Wait… What was her last name?

A smile overtook his features as he realized, for just a moment, that he had started to forget.

"You okay over there?" Kristin asked, pulling him back to reality and the choices he actually needed to make instead of the hypothetical fantasy he had rolling through his mind right now.

"Just thinking that in any rescue situation, we instruct everyone to stay where they are, so they can be found. Yet, that is assuming we need *rescue*." His smirk returned as he played on her statement. "So, we got this."

Oh, those famous last words. Even as he spoke, he could hear the doom that could come.

He brushed off the feeling, though. If anyone could get themselves out of the woods, they were definitely the ones. There was nothing to worry about. Yes, there were bears and mountain lions, freak blizzards and freezing rain, and criminals and jaded mountain men with a hatred of outsiders. Oddly enough, none of those things scared him half as much as spending more time with a woman whom he felt undeniably attracted to and was totally off-limits. Fangs, hypothermia and bullets weren't half as painful as heartbreak.

Chapter Six

The man was a walking red flag. Kristin had
no business noticing the way his eyes crinkled
just so when he smiled over at her, or the way
when he really laughed, he tipped back his head
ever so slightly. *No business.*

Even if she wanted to think about how sexy
he was, she had a job to do. Not to mention
the fact that they were, in effect, stranded in
the woods. It struck her as a little funny that
she was more worried about being so close to
this man when she should have been focused
on their life-and-death situation.

She spent the first mile walking in front of
him and as she stepped over the fallen timber
and through the thickets of willows in creek bottoms, she was more than certain she could feel
the weight of his gaze on her ass. Or maybe it
was her simply hoping that he was busy staring at her.

She wasn't the kind of woman to seek vali-

dation and value based on the attention and attraction levels of a man, but she yearned for his
interest nonetheless. What was wrong with her?

Pausing, she pulled up the map of the area
on her phone. She had a pretty good idea where
they were and how they needed to get out—it
was another ten miles west through some rough
terrain.

"So we are here," she said, pointing haphaz-
ardly at her phone.

He took her phone and zoomed in on the map.
"I think if we follow some of the game trails,
those will be our best bet. We need to avoid
this area here." He pointed at an area of steep
topography, which indicated a sharp drop-off.
"Yet, even if we go around, it's going to be some
tough going. Are you sure you don't want to
wait?"

"Absolutely not. It's dangerous going, but this
is the best option." The thought of sitting and
waiting was torturous. It may have been partly
ego and partly the fear of inadequacy, but she
couldn't be idle. Besides, if they waited, she
would be forced to talk to him more and that
would only lead to a deeper bond.

"The best option would have been to have a
working helo, but I hear what you're saying,"
he teased.

"Do you want to lead the pack?" she asked.

He nodded and brushed against her. As he did, she noticed a long cut on his arm. A gasp escaped her.

"Why didn't you tell me you were hurt?" She shrugged off her backpack and pulled out her medical kit before he even spoke.

"What?" He looked down his body, assessing himself.

"Your arm," she said, pointing at the bloody gash on the back of his left arm.

He lifted his arm, gazed at his wound. "Well, hell…"

"Where else are you hurt?" she asked, realizing now that while he had checked on her, she had failed to do the same to him.

Maybe she was more selfish than she had ever realized—not that her exes hadn't accused her of it before. Her last boyfriend and the SAR pilot, Greg, had been more than happy to point out every one of her seeming faults. His constant critique of everything that made her who she was—even down to how she always wore white socks instead of socks that matched her clothing—had directly led to their breakup.

Devaluing in a relationship was a real thing. Her therapist had talked to her about it, at length. Men and women who started to fall out of love, or who wanted to fall out of love, often tore down the person they were with in order to emotionally distance themselves. It was Psychology 101, but it hadn't made it any easier to live through or endure.

Though she couldn't have proven it, she had always felt Greg had been stepping out from their relationship. He would hide his phone and take late-night calls that he would give her vague answers about when she questioned his actions. She could have sworn that he had even flirted with her best friend, but he had brushed her off, claiming he was just being friendly.

Just thinking about having a boyfriend made her want to call her therapist and have her remind her of all the reasons she needed to get out of the woods and away from the man she was finding herself wholly attracted to, gash and all.

She grabbed the saline wash and cleaned the wound on his arm. He didn't flinch as she dabbed at his skin and then pitched the stained rag into a Ziploc bag and back into her pack. "What did you catch your arm on?" She took out a bottle of hydrogen peroxide as she spoke. "Did you cut it on the bird?"

He shook his head. "I have no idea." He glanced back over his shoulder at the stand of timber they had just come through. "I have a feeling I may have torn it up coming through there. I gotta admit that I may not have been totally paying attention to where I was walking when I was following you." There was an edge of joy in his tone.

She was more than aware of the next steps in this dance. If she asked him why he wasn't paying attention, it would open up their friendship to something *more*; and if she two-stepped around that, it would likely be the end of any further flirtation…*maybe*. That is, if she was reading it all right. As adept at relationships and flirting as she was, she could have been completely off base in how she was seeing this—it had been a while since she'd danced, figuratively or otherwise.

As quickly as she could, she dressed the wound. He would be fine, but there were a couple of spots that looked as though they would benefit from a stitch. She zipped her bag and tossed it back over her shoulder. "If we're going to make it out of the woods further unscathed, we both probably need to be extra vigilant."

As if he was oblivious to her warning, he walked up beside her, his uninjured arm brushing against her and making her skin spark to life.

Why did he have to go and do that? He wasn't making it any easier to push him away, when he literally wouldn't even stay at arm's length.

"How long have you been doing FLIR?" he asked.

Their footfalls crunched on the dirt path that was just wide enough for two people. "I dunno, a few years."

"How did you get started in it?" he asked.

She appreciated his attempt at small talk since it kept her from thinking so much about how he smelled of hydraulic fluid and sweat—a heady combination if ever there was one… If danger and sexiness had a trademark aroma, it would have definitely been this.

"I have always really been a tech girl, and imaging technology specifically. I was the girl who was studying radar signatures as a kid." She chuckled. "My parents never really understood what I found so fascinating, but they were super supportive. I can't tell you the number of times I made them watch the show *Radar Men from the Moon* from the 1950s. It was *awful*, but my grandfather got me started. We would sneak away to his den and watch the show."

"So you'd say that your entire life has been built on a kitschy show?"

"Not just that one," she said with a laugh, though she tried to watch her footing as they started to move into denser forest. "Basically, anything with talk of going to outer space and Martians…and I was all in. It was silly."

"That's not silly. It's pretty cool, actually.

Plus, it sounds like you have a really great grandfather."

"I did," she said, smiling at the memory of the man who had helped bring her up. "I went to his house every Sunday to help him with his yard in the summer and then his housework in the winter. Basically, though, we'd just have milk and cookies while we watched movies and talked football."

"So you're a football fan as well?"

"I loved the movies more, but I did learn enough about football to know that Joe Montana is the best football player who ever lived. Most people would disagree and say it's Tom Brady, thanks to his million and one Super Bowl wins, but Montana played in a time with less rules and when the game was far more physical."

He started to laugh. "That is one hell of a contentious opinion. Your grandfather sounds like he did a good job with you."

"Oh, my grandfather's more of a Namath fan. I'm a Montana girl, through and through." She chuckled.

"You're definitely that. Even if I don't agree with your taste in football players."

"Oh, you don't agree?" She grinned. "Don't tell me you are a Brady fan."

"I never said anything of the sort," he said, looking affronted.

"Don't start hedging your bets and laying up just because..." She paused, questioning whether or not she should say what she was thinking.

"Because why?" Casper asked, giving her a cheeky grin. "Why do you think I'd hold up?"

She readjusted the straps of her backpack on her shoulders, like they were the source of the additional weight she was feeling. "I think it's because you want me to like you."

He slowed down slightly, but she kept the same pace, leaving him behind her. A knot formed in her stomach. What if she had gotten her assumption wrong?

If she was in for a penny, at this point, she was in for a pound.

"Am I wrong?" She looked over her shoulder at him.

He was opening and closing his mouth like he was trying to get the right words out, but was failing.

"In all honesty, I didn't think that having a friendship with you was something that was really on the table."

She looked away, forced to pay attention to her footfalls on the trail as they started to ascend the mountain in front of them. She hated that she couldn't look at him while he was talking to her, but at the same time felt like it was silly she even had that thought.

"Why would you think friendship with me was off the table?"

"I'm sure you don't really want me to remind you, but…" he said, and jabbed his thumb in the direction they had come from.

"Unless you did that on purpose, which I'm fairly certain you didn't, then I'm going to say accidents happen and will leave it at that. No hard feelings." She paused as she thought about their first meeting and all the reasons he could have hated her. From his lack of response, she wondered if he was thinking about it as well. "If anything, I'm the one who should really feel bad. It was my inability to find your father sooner that may have resulted in his death."

"Don't even say that." He moved to her side and touched her shoulder, motioning for her to stop.

She turned to face him, but tried to look away. "Yes?"

He lifted her chin with his finger, forcing her to gaze up at him. "My father being out there and missing was no fault of yours. I hope you haven't been holding on to that all this time. If I am to blame anyone, I blame my brother and his wife." He looked her deep in the eyes, like he was trying to gauge her reaction and decide whether or not she believed him.

It didn't matter what he said—she would always feel like she hadn't acted quickly enough. It would be one of the incidents in this job that would haunt her for the rest of her career...if not her life.

"Do you know how far my father walked before you found him?"

She chewed on the inside of her cheek as she thought of the incident management plan her team had created before they had gone to search for the man. "He had last been seen by a hiker. They were the ones who called us and helped us to isolate his last known location."

"Who called to tell you he was missing?"

"I think it was the hiker, at least that's what I remember them saying in the briefing before the mission." She started to breathe harder as her body pushed to stay in pace with him as they worked their way up the mountain and toward the next ridgeline.

Casper simply nodded.

Her legs were burning and she let him move ahead of her as the trail narrowed and they gained elevation. Roots were sticking up out of the ground, forcing her to pick her steps carefully as she moved steadily up the mountain.

They had to have gone at least a mile, crawling over half-down logs and pushing through the bushes, which clung to her like they wanted her to stay in the woods forever. She could make out the sounds of Casper's heavy breaths in front of her. Her mind wandered as she tried to focus on something other than the tightness that was moving up from her calves and starting to twist through her thighs.

If she was already this tired so early in their hike, she would have to be careful not to hurt herself. Weariness led to accidents, and accidents to death.

Her GPS messenger pinged with a text.

"Casper," she called out, and he stopped. She took out the phone and clicked on the screen. He walked back and stepped beside her. "Cindy wants to know if she needs to send a team to intercept. She is concerned for our safety."

"At least she didn't tell me I'm fired." He gave her a weak smile, one that made her wonder exactly what all was on his mind.

"Can she fire a volunteer?"

He chuckled, but the sound was hard and dry. "If I was still in my old job, my ass would be gone. I'd be sitting at my commanding officer's desk and waiting for my formal investigation and write-up."

"You're a veteran?" She had always thought he was hot, but seeing him from this aspect made him seem just that much sexier—not only was he a pilot, but he was also a military man. For some reason, she ached to see him in uniform. A uniform that she could promptly rip off.

"Army. I was a member of the 160th. SOAR."

Yep. Just like that he went from a ten to an impossible eleven on the hotness scale.

"So you were a Night Stalker?"

He sent her a devilish grin. "You've heard of us?"

It could have been the stress of the hike, but her heart fluttered in her chest as his gaze seemed to penetrate straight to the center of her. "Uh-huh." She swallowed hard as she tried to gain control over her body. "Who in our world hasn't? You are the best of the best."

"Clearly, that can't be true. I just dropped us out of the sky, but I appreciate your belief in me." He laughed. "I have a feeling that when we get out of the woods, Cindy will be waiting and I will be the first chief warrant officer to be let go from a volunteer piloting position." He ran his hand over his face. "I can't wait to hear what my buddies will have to say."

"You don't think she will really let you go, do you?"

He scowled. "I potentially just lost my team hundreds of thousands of dollars…not to mention your crew as well. Your bird is laid up.

What if someone needs you? I may have just cost someone like my father their life."

She reached out and touched his arm. He was sweating from their hike and his muscles were pressing against his shirt. She shouldn't have touched him—it only made her attraction for him grow. "What happened out here, it wasn't your fault. If someone needs us, there are options..." Yet, even as she spoke, she couldn't deny he was right—this accident could very well end up costing more than either of them could imagine.

Chapter Seven

It was a crazy-ass feeling to come out of a life-and-death situation and wish that he could return to the uncertainty. Though Casper hoped Cindy would be understanding that what had happened was outside of his control, he wasn't sure the same could be said for the rest of the SAR unit. If he was turned away from his role in search-and-rescue, he would have nothing left. His entire identity would be stripped away and he would be left as an empty shell of the man he had once been.

He'd be nothing. He'd have *nothing*.

Though he wasn't the kind to give up at the first sign of adversity, he didn't have a backup plan for his life if everything fell through any more than it already had. Retiring from the military early had not done him any favors.

Kristin paused as he stopped to take a breath. The night was falling upon them and there was a bite to the air that promised frost.

"You going to be okay?" she asked, almost as if she could read his mind, or perhaps his body language.

"Am I that obvious?" He sighed.

She reached over and took his hand, lacing her fingers between his. "You saved my life. You know I'm going to have your back, no matter what happens down there."

At the edge of the timberline below them, in the valley bottom, there were the sounds of vehicles coming and going from their incident command center. Voices were carrying, but he couldn't make out words, only the manic tone of chaos.

He and Kristin had thrown the entire team on their ear.

Though he was grateful she had faith that he would make it through the investigation and ensuing debriefing without getting laid out, he wasn't about to point out the fact that she was probably wrong. And he *really* didn't want to talk about his feelings, or why he felt as he did and was so afraid.

So what if they had nearly died together? That certainly didn't mean he was ready to be *vulnerable*.

"Casper, we don't have to go down there and face the world until you are ready," Kristin continued, her voice soft.

He both liked and hated that she could be so understanding. They hardly knew each other, but it was like she could see right through him, and damn if it didn't jar him even more than the crash.

She leaned into him and put her head against his shoulder.

"You are a great woman," he said, leaning his head on top of hers.

Her hair smelled of sweat, fresh air and sunshine, and the effect was intoxicating. It struck him how something, some little action like this—one of kindness and understanding—could calm the storm within him. Whatever was to come would come, but at least in these few moments before he would have to face the crushing waves of questions and possible accusations, he had found a safe harbor.

Without thinking, he turned slightly and kissed the top of her head, pulling the scent of her deep into his lungs, as if this moment was the last peace he would find before his life fell apart. She gently moved back and looked up at him.

Their eyes met and he stared into the calming green he found. He had noticed her eyes before, but now it was like he was seeing them for the first time. Or, perhaps, it was that they were truly finally seeing one another. Until this moment, they had been forced to be together. As soon as they stepped back into the real world, they might not ever have to be this close again.

He had to take his chance. Yet, before he could move, Kristin lifted to her tiptoes and her lips met his. This time, she was the one who breathed him in, and the whisper of her breath matched perfectly with the soft, yearning tempo of her kiss.

Until now, he hadn't realized that he was the one who needed to be saved…but mostly from himself and the battles within his mind.

The kiss was gentle and as full of grace and tenderness as Kristin. She let her lips linger against his and then touched her forehead to his, the simple act as sexy and sweet as the kiss. What he would give to be with a woman like her.

"I'm your ally. No matter what happens down there, I won't let you take the fall." She brushed the back of his hand with hers as she moved away from him. "When you are ready…" She waved in the direction of the camp.

"In case I don't get to say this later, thank you." He smiled at her, but even he could feel the tiredness in his eyes.

It was matched in hers. "Save your thanks until we are through this."

He touched her shoulder as he moved by her. "Let's go rip this Band-Aid off."

BY THE TIME they reached the camp, the light had faded from the sky and everyone in the camp had heard about their mishap. He and Kristin walked by the helo pad where his bird rested. There was a cacophony of voices coming from inside the different tents, but no one seemed to be outside. He was relieved no one had the chance to stop them as they made their way inside the wall tent that stood at the heart of the camp. Cindy was sitting in a folding chair at the main table sipping a cup of coffee and staring down at a topographic map like it held all the answers they needed.

"The party has arrived!" Casper called, slapping the guy nearest to him on the back as he made his way inside.

Kristin didn't recognize the man, but her friend, and the regular pilot of the helo, was sitting two seats down in another folding chair. He turned toward her and his face was tight. He quickly looked away, though she couldn't imagine why. Perhaps he was upset with the crash, or he felt as if he was somehow culpable in what had transpired. She would definitely need to deal with him later—she could hardly wait.

"Get your asses up here." Cindy pointed at the open seats at the table, and while her action was authoritarian and ordering, there was undeniably relief in her tone.

Forcing herself to ignore the urge to slink toward the woman in charge, Kristin straightened her back and readied herself to go to the gallows at Casper's side. He couldn't be blamed for what had happened.

Cindy said something behind her hand to the man to her left before turning to the rest of the people who had gathered around. "Hey, guys," she called loudly, "we appreciate all your efforts in making sure that Kristin and Casper arrived safely back at the camp as well as taking care of the teams. However, we will need anyone who isn't one of the board members to leave the area for a bit…until we have gone over what transpired."

There was a collective grumble and a few choice words that Kristin could hear whispered under breaths. If all these folks had been a part of their return, she could understand their reticence in being sent from the room at such a pivotal moment.

"Yeah, yeah… Keep your griping to yourselves." Cindy pointed toward the door. "There is a food truck outside with some damned good barbeque. Eat and we will meet back up in an hour."

The pilot bumped against her shoulder, almost knocking her off balance. "Greg?" Kristin asked.

He didn't look at her and instead barreled outside and into the night.

"Damn, he is charming," Casper said, nudging his chin toward the guy. "Should I be jealous?" He smiled.

"Greg isn't like that, *usually*." She looked back over her shoulder in the direction in which her ex-boyfriend had disappeared.

"Casper. Kristin. We're waiting." Cindy lost any softness that had been in her voice earlier, when she had first seen them.

Casper let out a long exhale before making his way to the table with her at his heels.

She wanted to speak up. To intercede and tell Cindy and the other three lieutenants sitting at the table that this had merely been an accident… Really, they had made it out of the woods almost unscathed.

"First things first," Cindy began. "I can't tell you how relieved I am. We *all* are—" she motioned to the camp "—that you have made it back. We had a pool going whether or not we would have to come in with a stretcher."

Casper chuckled. "I'm glad to hear that you guys didn't let an opportunity to gamble on our welfare pass you by."

"Are you saying you wouldn't have done the same thing if you knew I was accounted for and healthy, but needing to self-rescue my ass from the woods?" Cindy laughed.

"When you put it like that, I think I would have doubled down," Casper said, the aluminum folding chair scraping on the gravel on the ground of the tent and making a pinging sound. "Which side of the bet were you on?"

She waved him off with a laugh. "You know that I have the utmost faith in you... Even if you did crash a helicopter that didn't belong to our team and ruined our chances at funding."

The words coming out of her mouth and the tone of her voice were inconsistent. It sounded almost as if Cindy was empathetic and understanding about what had happened. Kristin had prepared herself for almost every possible scenario with Casper's team and what would happen in this moment, but she hadn't accounted for this possibility.

She glanced over at Casper and he looked as utterly confused as she was feeling.

"Kristin," Cindy said, turning to her, "I must offer my sincere apologies. I'm sure that we will get to the bottom of what happened and why. In the meantime, we will make sure that you and your pilot will be taken care of and have anything you need to make it back to Billings safely."

"Thank you," she said, sounding almost

breathless. "I… I'm going to need to get our mechanics out here."

"Greg, your pilot, said he would take care of things."

At least someone knew what was going on.

"Good. Glad to hear he is on top of things."

"As for what happened, you have stated in your texts that you believe none of what happened was due to negligence on Casper's part. Am I correct in this?"

She had the sickening feeling that she had suddenly found herself in the court of Judge Cindy and she was front and center on the witness stand. Though she wasn't exactly sure of what she should say that would keep her lawyers happy, but she had made a vow to Casper and she intended on keeping it.

"From what I witnessed, there was a critical hydraulic leak. Your pilot, Mr. Keller, did a commendable job in bringing us down in a safe and effective way even though the environment around us didn't lend itself toward success. I would go so far as to say that Casper saved our lives."

Cindy sent her a wide smile.

"Now, if you don't mind, I need to talk to my pilot and make sure we have everything in order to get our helo back and in working order. We have lives to save."

Casper ran his hand over her lower back and the simple action made a warmth roll through her body.

Apparently, she had passed the questioning with flying colors. Better—in doing so, she had also fulfilled her promise…at least for now. As it stood, the future was in their hands.

Chapter Eight

Greg had no real excuse to act as he had, at least not as far as Kristin was concerned. The man had known the risks that always went with flying. No pilot was immune to the inevitability that at some point or another, they would go down. If anything, he should have been glad that the helo would probably come through this event to fly another day and he hadn't been the one on the stick.

She, on the other hand, couldn't say she was raring to jump back into a bird.

Regardless, she needed to get to the bottom of what, exactly, was getting to him the most about the accident. If everything went her way, maybe she could talk him down off the ledge and perhaps even turn this melee into a positive. She definitely wasn't sure how she would go about that, even though she had been trying to come up with something the entire hike back. Every time she tried to focus on the political game, which would have to be played once they returned, all she could focus on was Casper and the way his voice made her body clench.

He was not good for her attention span or capacity for critical thinking. Damn him. Or, maybe, damn her for being so at mercy to her baser needs. She was a professional woman, and as soon as she got back to her desk at FLIR Tech, she would have plenty of time to think about Casper's round, bounce-a-quarter-off-it ass.

At the mere thought of what she had just said to herself, she ran a hand over her face.

Here, she had been thinking that the hardest part of the wreck was already over—they had landed it and self-rescued. Never had she thought the assuaging of feelings and tiptoeing through confusing politics would be the hardest part.

Casper was still in the tent with Cindy, and she was grateful, as it would give her the chance to come back to her senses and ground herself in reality.

She made her way toward the food truck, where she hoped to find Greg. He couldn't have gone far, as they didn't have any private area or tent that she was aware of; though, she doubted from the look on his face when she'd last seen him that eating was at the forefront of his mind, but if he wasn't there, she could expand her search as need required.

She chuckled at the thought of how all day she had been searching for something, and even at camp, she was on the hook. Truth be told, though, she kinda loved every second of it. It was a hell of a thing to be needed—more, required.

When she and Greg had been dating, most of the time he could have been best described as indifferent. Maybe that was what was bothering him. He was jealous of her spending time in the air with Casper, or maybe he was just mad that she was finally moving on.

Nah. That couldn't have been it. They had been broken up for more than three months.

Thinking back, it might have been even longer than that. It was Greg who had informed her that he was going to start seeing other people. She'd agreed and he had left her with the old cliché—"Don't worry, we can still be friends." It was in that moment she had been more sure than ever that he had already been sleeping with other women. It sucked knowing she hadn't been enough for him.

As if Greg could sense that she was replaying their relationship of convenience in her mind, he stepped out from behind the tent nearest the food truck. He was holding a white foam container, and even from here, she could smell the Cholula hot sauce and barbecue sauce. She liked both things, but couldn't wrap her head around why he would want to ruin two great condiments by mixing them together.

Yeah…there was no denying her feelings for him were solidly dead if she could dislike everything about him down to the way he ate.

"Greg, you have a minute to chat?" she called to him.

He looked up from picking at his food and popped a piece of what looked like pulled pork into his mouth. "Whadya want?" he said, a tendril of pork sticking out of his mouth as he spoke.

Yep, he was gross. How had she ever been attracted to this guy?

"What just happened in there?" she asked, pointing vaguely in the direction of the main tent.

"Are you kidding me?" he asked, wiping at his mouth with the back of his hand as he finally remembered to swallow his bite.

"No. I thought we were fine. I thought we were getting along…and now you are throwing shoulders? What in the hell?" Her jaw hardened as she tried to control her bubbling anger at the man. She had gone to bat and called him a friend, and now he was treating her like this… *How dare he.*

He crushed the container in his hand. "You have, and will always be, one of the most self-centered people I've ever met." He walked toward the garbage can and threw away the box so hard it made the steel can ring.

His words made her take a quick inventory of her life. There were a number of incidents where she hadn't done her best, but she had always thought she had gone out of her way to not only care for her self-interest, but also for other's wishes, especially when it came to Greg. She had even gone so far as to take his mother to and from pretty much all of her doctor's appointments for six months because he was "too busy." That should have been a red flag, but apparently her dumb ass thought those flags were opportunities for a man to experience personal growth—growth she had once believed she was capable of inspiring.

What a fool she had been.

"I—I get that you think you have a right to be mad because your bird went down." She tried to stop the quaver that had somehow stupidly made its way into her voice. This wasn't the time to be weak. "However, you have no right to start attacking me—personally or professionally. You work *for* me."

His eyes grew wide, but his surprise rapidly turned into an angry scowl. "First, we both know you don't have the authority to fire me. Even if you did, don't think for a second that I can't blink and get another job."

"Don't think for a second that you're not replaceable."

The sound of his stupid laugh made the hair stand on her arms. "You are the one who is replaceable—not the other way around. What I do takes skill. Few are as good as me. As if I have to remind you that it was your new *buddy* who nearly killed you." He blew out a dismissive snort. "I bet FLIR already has applicants lined up for your easy gig."

It took everything in her power not to punch the smug look off his face. Even if it took every ounce of her willpower, as soon as they got back to Billings she would work on getting him relieved of duty. Good or not, he was not the best man for the job. Until then, however, if he wasn't going to quit on his own, they were going to have to get along.

"Look, we got off on the wrong foot here. Let's restart this whole thing. All I wanted to really know was whether or not you called in the mechanics. We need to get the bird out of the woods."

"If you hadn't signed us up for this stupid

training session, then *my bird* wouldn't be stranded out there in the first place. I hope you know that I'm holding you personally responsible."

She turned on her heel and did a quick about-face as she tried to hold in her rage in front of this shark.

There was being stupid and there was opening a vein in the water. This was her fault. She had foolishly thought that exes could be friends…or, at the very least, civil to each other.

Drawing in a breath, she turned back to him when she was just far enough away that her face could be masked by the darkness. "Greg, I hope you know you've become a man I wouldn't wish upon my worst enemies."

"It's funny," he said, his features hard, "I could almost say the same of you. In fact, you are dumber than a box of crayons and just about as useful. No one needs someone like you in their life—any woman is better than you."

Hot, angry tears filled her eyes. Fuming, she headed toward the main tent. Rounding a corner, someone grabbed her. Instinctively, she threw up her hands and felt her palm connect with a man's nose.

"Damn it!" Casper exclaimed, cupping his nose in his hands. "Why did you do that?"

"Oh… Oh, I'm so-o-o sorry. I…" She stumbled to find the right words. "I didn't know it was you. I just reacted."

"I heard you and Greg fighting and I was trying to come out to help." He tilted his head back in an attempt to staunch the stream of blood that was dripping down his chin.

Patting her pockets, she came to the one on her thigh and withdrew a black bandana. "Here," she said, gently swabbing at the blood on his chin before motioning for him to use it for his nose.

"Thanks." He took the cloth and dabbed at his nose before holding it still.

"So you heard all that, huh?" She nibbled at her lower lip.

He nodded.

"I'm guessing that everyone else did as well?"

"Without a doubt."

She ran her hands over her face and gave a long exhale. "Well, so much for coming off as professional."

"I think professional left the building when you punched me in the nose," he said with a laugh, but the sound was cut off as he winced in pain.

"Yeah, about that…" She cringed.

"If you were going to punch someone, you really should have made it Greg."

"Trust me, I wanted to punch him."

"So did I." He motioned in the dude's direction. "Want me to go do it now?"

"If I can kick your ass, I don't think you have a chance. Sorry." She laughed. "Seriously, though, thanks for trying to come to my defense, but all I'm going to really need is a drive back to Billings."

He motioned toward the helicopter on the pad. "I can do better..."

Chapter Nine

"I'm going to need to be talked into going back in the air," Kristin challenged, but there was a cute smirk on her face that said it wouldn't take too much convincing for her to come back up with him.

"Lucky for me, I have an ace in the hole." Casper lifted the cloth to reveal his blood. "You did just hit me in the nose."

She frowned, but the tremble in her lips gave away the fact she was trying to stop from smiling. "I don't think that really compares to you crashing us into the ground."

"*Crash* is such a strong word." He laughed, but stopped as the pain from his nose pinged through him. *Thinking about pain...* "So I'm assuming Greg is your ex?"

Now she was the one who looked like she was hurting, and he wished he hadn't brought up the obvious.

"I can't say that I want to talk about it, but,

yeah. Though, I would never have considered us to be in a real relationship."

"Was it you or him that didn't *define* what you had?" He was genuinely curious as to who she was in a partnership, the giver or the taker.

She quirked an eyebrow at him. "I never pushed and he never offered."

Kristin was definitely the giver.

He was a giver in relationships, too. Maybe that was another reason they couldn't really be anything besides a quick kiss in the woods and maybe a night or two in Billings before he returned to Big Sky. Yeah, they might see each other at a work function here or there, but the eight hours drive time between her home and his definitely put yet another damper on things between them.

Kristin sighed, signaling an end to any more questions about her ex. He didn't mind, though. There was nothing worse than talking about the past. At least, the painful moments. He had no desire to open up, give her the dirty details and talk about the times in life when he had been brought to his knees. They had already been through enough just in the last twenty-four hours, so going through another wave of emotions sounded like the next ascension in their levels of this hellish day.

"I bet you are exhausted. You camping here tonight?" he asked, motioning toward the tents.

She looked over her shoulder in the direction of where she had been talking to Greg outside the food truck. "We were going to grab a hotel."

Did that mean that she and Greg had planned on spending the night together? The thought made him surprisingly jealous. Now he was aching to ask her how long Greg had been her ex and what had happened to bring their *thing* together to an end, but it was conversation non grata.

Really, though, he reminded himself, *what does it matter?*

"If you want, I have a house with three bedrooms. You could help yourself to the spare."

"That would be great. I have my stuff in the helo…" She pointed in the direction of the helicopter pad, but then her arm fell. "Strike that— beyond what is in my backpack in the tent, I may need to stop and get a few things. Would you mind?"

"Not at all," he said. "If it's basic stuff, though, I have extras."

"In the event your girlfriend stays over or something?" she asked, but he could tell from her tone that it was more than just an attempt to be playful and she was really questioning him about his personal life.

"No girlfriend."

"Then why do you have a three-bedroom house with only one spare bedroom?"

He smirked. "You promise not to laugh at me?"

"Do you have a sex dungeon or something?" she teased. "If you do, you have to tell me now. I think that is legally required." She giggled.

How did one little sound make him want to pull her into his arms and kiss her again?

"I don't know what kind of guy you think I am, but if I'm single, I feel like a sex dungeon might be a bit of a waste of space."

"If being an adult has taught me anything, it is that regardless of relationship statuses, sex happens."

She had clearly been broken by men in her past. Maybe being broken by exes was something they could have in common.

He paused for a moment. Was all this sex talk implying that she would be interested in spending the night with him in more than a spare-bedroom kind of way? Though he wanted to clarify things between them to a certain extent, asking her what she wanted from him tonight seemed like he would be taking things too close to *real* for his liking.

The thought made him laugh. Here they were,

talking about relationships, but asking her about what she wanted from him was *too real*.

"Sorry," she continued, seemingly uncomfortable with his silence. "I didn't mean to take things that far. I..." She swayed from foot to foot nervously. "That was all out of line."

"Kristin," he said, realizing that it was the first time he had spoken her name aloud and, secretly, he loved the way it felt rolling over his tongue. "You never have to apologize for talking to me. You're hilarious."

She turned her face slightly, hiding it from him as though she was blushing.

"I won't judge you as long as you don't judge me about my bedroom situation."

"Oh," she said, sounding relieved of her embarrassment, "are you going to tell me your deep, dark secret?"

He laughed. "It's not deep or dark, but I do have the most pampered dog on the entire planet." He glanced down at his watch. "Actually, I probably need to pick him up from the dog-sitter."

She gave a jovial laugh, but it was a light and loving sound. "Oh, my goodness. That may be the cutest thing you've said to me since we met." She paused. "What kind of dog is this prince or princess?"

"Prince. His name is Grover and he is a gold-endoodle. He's four and needs a lot of exercise."

"I can't wait to meet him. I *love* dogs." She put her hands to her mouth in excitement in a way that made him almost as excited as her. "I warn you now, though—you may not get him back. Dogs tend to adopt me as their people." They walked into the tent and she grabbed her bag as they spoke.

"I'm sure he is waiting impatiently to meet you," he said as they walked toward the parking lot and his waiting pickup.

She smiled at him as he opened up the door for her and she climbed inside. Before he got in, he took a long breath, trying to control the strange nervousness that was building within him. It was one thing to talk about her staying at his place overnight, but it was another thing entirely to actually make it happen.

He attempted to remind himself that he had no reason to feel like this—it wasn't as if they hadn't been alone all day. Yet, he kept circling back to the fact that this was *different*. Things between them had shifted with their kiss, and there was no going back and putting his attraction back on the shelf.

He glanced in the truck, and saw that she had pulled down the visor and was rubbing something beneath her eye. It made him wonder if she, too, was feeling the same kind of push and pull that he was. If anything, though, she seemed generally at ease with going home with him.

She had made it clear that she wasn't comfortable taking things between them toward sharing a bed.

He climbed into the truck as she closed the visor mirror and it slapped back into place.

"Yeah, I definitely look like I fell out of the sky today. It's a good thing you aren't taking me on a date."

He inadvertently jerked the wheel as they started down the road. Did she want to go on a date? Was that like a midwestern hint that she wanted him to take her out? Or was that a subtle strike into the friend zone? He wasn't sure he wanted to know, and he didn't want to have to play any more games.

"I have to say, I'm glad you know you can trust me." He smiled over at her, but what he really wanted to do was reach across the console and take her hand. He wanted to touch her so bad.

"What do you mean?"

"I just mean that in all reality we just met."

"Technically, we met a few weeks ago, but I know where you are going with this," she said, correcting him.

"True," he said with a little nod. "Yet, we really only talked for the first time today. I don't know many women who would feel comfortable going home with a guy the same day."

"You must not have ever gone drinking at a college-aged bar, then," she said with a laugh.

"Damn, you know what…? Now that I hear myself saying that out loud, I…" He laughed with her. "Seriously, though, I'm taking it as a compliment that you know you are safe with me."

"You're always a damned hero, aren't you?" she teased, her smile not wavering on her lips as she spoke.

He moved like he was going to grab something out of the back seat. "Ah, man…"

"What?" she asked, looking behind them. "Do you need me to grab something?"

He chuckled. "Nah, it just looks like I forgot to throw my superhero cape in the back seat again."

She gave him a playful nudge. "You are ridiculous. You know that, right?"

"I may be ridiculous, but I have a feeling that you may like it." He couldn't help himself—he extended his hand in the hope that she would slip her fingers between his.

He wasn't left disappointed when her warm

hand slipped in his and they interlaced their fingers. He could get used to having this beautiful woman at his side.

Chapter Ten

Grover was even cuter in person than Casper had described the dog. He jiggled and wiggled as his tail whipped back and forth and he pranced in excitement as she petted him. He looked so much like an apricot teddy bear, that if he had round ears he would have almost been a dead ringer for a stuffed animal... Well, one that whined to get scratches right at the base of his tail.

This combo of Casper and Grover proved that there was such a thing as immediately feeling at home.

"He is a charmer." Casper gave the dog a pat on the head as he led her down the hall and toward what she assumed were the bedrooms.

The house was nicer than she had thought it would be, not that she had really *expected* anything. Everything was in order, all the way down to the blanket that had been folded neatly over the leather couch in the living room when she had walked by.

"Do you have a housekeeper in addition to a dog-sitter?"

"Nah," he said, shaking his head. "I'm not really busy enough to need one. Plus, I enjoy taking care of things myself. I find that if I keep my boots on the ground, I have a better idea of what awaits me."

She wasn't sure she knew what exactly he was referring to when it came to *awaiting* things, but she assumed it probably had something to do with his time in the military. "Do you work in addition to volunteering for SAR?"

"I'm a trained mechanical engineer. I got my PhD in engineering while I was in the army. Lately, I've been doing some freelance stuff from home in my downtime. Mostly, I play with Grover and then SAR stuff. It doesn't sound like much, but I'm generally pretty busy."

She unintentionally scrunched her face at his words.

"You don't like that I have my PhD?" he teased.

Kristin touched the back of her hair, smoothing it as she glanced over at him. "No, that's not it at all."

"So I read you right—something is bothering you."

"It's just that," she continued, taking a breath as she weighed whether or not she truly wanted to say what she was thinking, "it sounds like you are really busy."

He put his hand on her lower back and the simple action soothed the compression in her chest. "Kristin…" He said her name like it was a prayer. "I am busy because it keeps me from thinking about the things that I don't have in my life."

She glanced down the hallway at several oil paintings of mountains and one of a moose that were hanging at the end of the long corridor. "Don't take this the wrong way, but it actually looks like you have everything you could want."

He gave her a sidelong glance. "That may be true when it comes to materialistic things, but over the last few years, after having retired from the army, I've just come to realize that what is important in life isn't the *stuff*." He started to walk down the hallway.

"Then what is important to you?" she asked, following him and ever so nonchalantly trying to catch a glimpse of his ass. It really was a thing of beauty, and she could definitely see it becoming something important to her.

Grover wagged his tail as he meandered up beside her and leaned against her leg, then glanced at her like he had caught her checking him out and was now hoping for pets, as if they were some sort of blackmail for his not telling. The word *cheeky* came to mind as she scratched the dog's head.

"You may think I'm trying to blow smoke up your dress, but I've got to say that the most important things in life are the relationships which you build and devote yourself to."

"So, family?"

He huffed. "I would like to agree with that, but my family is a bit of a mess. I'd hate for others to define me or judge me based on their behavior. Though…" He paused as Grover pranced over to him and looked at his master with his tongue lolling out of his mouth. "I would make an exception when it came to my mom and dad. They were good people."

"You mentioned you had a brother. Is it just the two of you?"

He nodded. "William and his wife, Michelle. They don't have any kids yet, but I know they have been trying."

"Are you close with them?"

There was something about the way his eye twitched when she asked that told her there was a lot of unpacking that would have to be done when it came to the subject of his brother and his wife.

"It's *tenuous*."

From his clipped response, he wasn't ready to talk about them. She hoped it was because he was having fun with her that made him reticent to open up and not that he wasn't willing to be himself with her.

He stopped beside the first bedroom door on his left. Inside was a beautiful queen-size bed with an antique-looking white bedspread. It was the heavy kind with lace tatting on the edges. In the corner of the room was a treadle Singer sewing machine. If she had been given a lifetime to guess what was in his guest room, the last thing she would have guessed would have been a shabby-chic throwback that she might have expected to see in a bed-and-breakfast.

Stepping into the room, she was actually impressed. There was a bookshelf against the wall filled with everything from Austen and Brontë, to Stoker and Poe. "You have all of my favorites covered," she said, motioning toward the shelves. "I've always believed you can safely judge a person by what they enjoy reading."

He gave her a guilty look. "While I have read some of those," he began, "I have to own up to the fact that this house used to belong to my parents. This was my mother's stuff."

She paused, trying to reconcile herself to the fact that this handsome man had not only kept his mother's things on display, but had also welcomed her into this place filled with mementos that clearly must have meant something to him. Some of her friends may have hated this kind of thing, but it had been a rarity in her life to meet a man with an emotional range larger than a toothpick.

"This is make-or-break," she said, smiling at him as she kidded around. "Austen or Brontë?"

He walked over to the bookshelf and pulled out *Jane Eyre* and *Emma*, but left *Pride and Prejudice* sitting lonely in the corner. It pulled at her, as if he had done something profane, and she moved to pick it up.

"Hey, now," he said, stopping her gently with an outstretched hand. "What do you think you are doing?"

She pointed at her favorite book and gave him doe eyes. "No one leaves Elizabeth Bennet in the corner."

He laughed at her. "I should have known you were a romance fan."

"What is that supposed to mean?" she asked, slightly worried about her fantasy world, where he was the one straight man on the planet who not only understood the Elizabeth Bennet reference, but also appreciated the works for the glorious keystones of romance that they were.

"I just mean that all the best women have a thing about romance novels." He smiled. "Hear me out, but I have always found that all my exes who enjoyed reading romances were the most open-minded and sexually free lovers I've ever had."

"Oh, you've had a lot of lovers, have you?" Jealousy flashed through her.

"Not where I was going with that at all. And, no." He slipped his hand in hers, but as he did, Grover nudged them to pet him and she was forced to oblige.

"Grover is jealous." She scratched behind his ear as he gazed up at her.

"I don't think he is the only one," Casper said. "Seriously, I hope you know that there is nothing to worry about when it comes to that kind of thing. I'm a one-woman man when I'm in a relationship, or even a *situationship.*"

She wanted to ask him if that was what he could see them becoming, but at the same time, she didn't want to press the issue. They could have this night and maybe a few more days together, but their time this close to one another was preciously limited. She didn't want a long-distance thing or even a situationship. If she was going to give her heart to another, she wanted to give it all, without reservation.

"I will set things out in the bathroom in the hall for you," he continued, as though he could pick up on the fact that their conversation had pulled out feelings within her that she couldn't reconcile. "If you need anything, I'm down at the end of the hall. It's the door on the left. Grover's door is on the right. Just so you know, you got the larger bedroom." He smiled, but there was something in his eyes that spoke of his holding something back.

"Thank you, Casper," she said.

"It's my pleasure. And I hope you know, I won't try and put you in danger again," he said, giving her a look so sweet and kind that she yearned to touch him, but if she touched him, she wasn't sure she could stop her hands from slipping down to his round ass.

Grover definitely wouldn't approve.

"I appreciate that." She couldn't help but feel like his keeping her out of danger was one thing he couldn't promise.

Casper looked nervous as he moved toward the door. "Again, if you need anything..." He gestured vaguely in the direction of his bedroom. "Night." He paused for a second and his hand started to move toward her, but he stopped himself and instead turned on his heel, like he had thought better of reaching out for her. The door gently clicked shut behind him.

Disappointment swelled within her, but in its wake was a strange sense of gratitude. There was something inexplicably sweet about this man who didn't encroach on her boundaries or make her uncomfortable. She appreciated it, but in other circumstances, she would have wished he'd have pressed her up against the wall and taken what they both wanted.

It didn't take long for her to take a shower. Luckily, she always packed a change of clothes in her go bag, but they had been packed away inside it for so long that they had a strange, musty aroma, like they had been sweaty and dried several times thanks to her many adventures trudging them around. She shrugged off the odor—it didn't really matter what she smelled like. It wasn't like anyone was going to be close enough to her to notice. Yet, she thought better of wearing them as they were.

After wrapping the towel from her shower tightly around her, she put her phone in her pocket and picked up the clothes she'd been wearing and walked them down to the laundry. It felt weird using his house like it was her own, but if they were going to be together again all day tomorrow, she needed to get cleaned up so she wouldn't be putting herself in a situation where she would be even more uncomfortable or ill-at-ease than she already was. She needed to bring her A game.

After putting her clothes in the washer, she was met with the *click-click-click* sound of Grover's nails on the tile outside the door in the hall. He came around the corner, stuck his head in and gave her what she could have best described as a dog smile.

"Hey-a, buddy," she said, pouring the soap into the machine and then reaching over to pet the dog.

His tail thumped against the doorjamb as he moved closer to her. She started the wash and then kneeled down to give Grover some proper attention. Her towel shifted slightly, opening at the bottom, and she tried to move it closed, but it didn't really matter if the dog saw her thigh, so she conceded the battle.

"He really is the world's worst guard dog," Casper said, stepping into view at the door to the laundry room.

She jerked slightly, reaching to close her towel as she stood up, but in doing so she loosened the knot at the top and it slipped, almost exposing her nipples. Thankfully, she grabbed it just in time, but she wasn't sure exactly how much Casper had gotten to see of her naked body.

She flushed with embarrassment. "I—I…" she stammered. "He is." She sounded breathless. "I hope it's okay that I'm using your washer, I just needed…" Feeling stupid for explaining the working of a washing machine, she stopped herself.

Casper's gaze was steadfast on her face, like he had maybe seen more than she had hoped, and was now concentrating as hard as he could on not trying to make her feel embarrassed about the slip.

"You... You can do whatever you like," Casper said, his stare even more pronounced than it had been, like he was afraid to blink. "I mean...my house is your house."

He may have been even more embarrassed than her, and she found it to be endearing. She moved closer to him as the washing machine started to fill with water and the sound echoed through the small room. Grover moved out of her way, disappearing into the hallway.

Lightening her tight hold on her towel, she let it sink a little lower on her sides, exposing her pale skin. Casper's gaze shifted downward, but then shot back up. Moving even closer, she could hear his erratic breathing. She kept inching nearer, ever so slowly, almost timid. She waited for his consent, but was steady in her progression toward him.

"Casper," she said softly, as she hoped he saw the want for him in her eyes. "I know we haven't really talked about what we want...*from each other*. We have, but...well, you know."

He didn't say a word and stood as though he was afraid if he moved, she would dart away.

"I know it's not possible for us to be in a real relationship, but what if we treat this night as a one-time thing. We can go back to working together in the morning." Even as she spoke, she knew her idea was far-fetched and idealistic at best, but they had already taken one step into the realm of awkwardness. What were another few leaps?

She extended her fingers, brushing the backs of them against his in a silent question. He answered by wrapping his fingers through hers and bringing them to his mouth, softly kissing their embracing hands. His lips were hot against her skin, but his breath was even hotter. Something about the cadence of his kisses and the lust-filled look in his eyes made it obvious that he wanted her as much, if not more, than she wanted him.

He took her other hand and pulled it gently away from where it held her towel in place. The white cotton cloth fell to a heap on the floor, but Casper didn't look down at her nakedness. Instead, he wrapped his arms behind her back and pressed her body against his. Melding her lips with his, he kissed her like she had never been kissed before. His body grew hard against her.

His kiss deepened as he pulled her hands tighter behind her, her shoulders constricted and her body grew wet in anticipation of his touch.

Leaning back, she lifted her chin and his kiss moved down the skin of her neck. "Casper," she moaned.

"Mmm-hmm," he said, moving his kisses lower until he found her nipple and he drew it into his mouth and gently sucked.

"That feels... So... Good."

He let go of her hands and took hold of each side of her hips. He gripped her as if he wanted to kiss every inch of her until there was no part of her left untouched. She clenched and ached with want. His lips glided over her as he moved lower and lower between her legs, taking his time in the descent, and into the madness that came with making love.

Now on his knees, he stopped kissing and looked up at her. Their gazes met and she sent him a dazed smile. She would be happy if this could be her forever, but for now, she would merely be euphorically satisfied.

There was a buzz as her phone rang. She tried to ignore it, holding Casper's head gently as to keep him from moving away from her, but it was of no use. "You should answer that," Casper said, stopping and looking up at her.

She gave an audible groan. "I'm sorry. There're not very many people that I have on bypass. Usually, my phone never rings. When it does, it has to be something important."

"You know I understand," Casper said, kissing her stomach gently as he rose to his feet.

The phone buzzed again and she begrudgingly turned away and picked up the offending device.

Greg.

She could only imagine what he wanted, but just seeing his name pissed her off. She couldn't believe she had forgotten to demote his call-bypass status when they had broken up.

"What?" she answered angrily.

"What the hell do you think you are doing?" he yelled into the phone, making her pull it away from her ear.

"What are you talking about?" she asked, her eyes darting to Casper.

"I can't believe you went home with the pilot. What are you thinking? You have no right leaving me here at camp while you go out and are—"

She lowered the phone, aware that only a line of expletives would be following in his tirade.

From the wide-eyed look on Casper's face, he could hear Greg. She mouthed *I'm sorry.* Casper, waving her off, grabbed her towel and handed it to her, then motioned that he would wait outside.

She tried to indicate that he should stay, but he was insistent and he quickly made his way out of the room while she ignored the berating coming from the other end of the line.

As the door clicked shut, she turned her attention back to the abusive jerk who was still yelling.

"Listen, Greg, I don't need to hear from you right now. This isn't an emergency and I'm not accountable to you. I'm not your subordinate or your girlfriend." Ire rose within her. "Regardless of what role you think you play in my life, you have no right to treat me like this. We will discuss this tomorrow, when I'm back at work."

She hung up the phone.

She clicked on his name, then blocked him.

Wrapping the towel back around her, she walked out of the room, but Casper had disappeared. She paused as she looked up and down the hallway, waiting to hear the click of the dog's nails, or Casper calling her name, but she was only met with silence.

Though she wanted things to continue as they had been with Casper, Greg had killed the mood. If she went to Casper now, things would be weird and she would have to explain more about her former relationship with Greg.

As the flush from Casper's kisses started to fade, logical thought flowed back into her.

Maybe Greg-the-ass had really done her a favor. His ill-timed and kiss-blocking call may have just saved her from a future heartbreak.

Chapter Eleven

Grover wagged his tail hard against the seat as Casper pulled into the house with fresh coffee and croissants. He had a few things in his house, but he assumed Kristin needed a little bit of privacy to get ready for the day and he could probably earn a few bonus points by bringing her the best coffee in town.

As he put the truck in Park, Kristin came rolling outside. Grover stood up, his tail moving faster, and he started whining as he waited for her to walk over to them.

"Where have you been?" she asked, her voice a mix of annoyance and what he guessed was fear.

"Don't worry, we didn't leave you. Just wanted to get some breakfast."

She opened up the truck door and Grover assaulted her with licks.

"Grover, no. Get in the back," he ordered the dog, who gave him an annoyed look before jumping over the console and into the back seat. "Sorry about that, he was missing you this morning. It took everything in my power to get him not to scratch at your door until you woke up. He has no manners."

"Are we dropping him off at the sitter's?" Kristin asked, jumping in the truck.

In all actuality, he hadn't planned on leaving as soon as he got back with coffee. If he had his way, they would have picked up where they had left off last night, right before her ex had decided to butt back into her life. They way Greg had sounded on the phone had kept him awake for hours last night, wondering if they were as over as she had said they were. From the guy's annoyance, it seemed like he thought he still had a chance of getting back into Kristin's private life.

Casper wasn't perfect by any means, and he had said any number of stupid things when talking to women he cared for, but he'd never broken down or disrespected a woman he had loved, even after a breakup. He always believed that just because a relationship hadn't worked, it didn't mean the woman he'd been attracted to wasn't a good person... She just wasn't the person for him. This *vaya-con-Dios* attitude had left him with most of his exes still considering him as a friend.

Kristin had said she considered Greg a friend, but if those were the kinds of friends she had… well, she could do better.

She clicked her seat belt and Casper handed her the breakfast he had brought. "I was thinking we could bring him along. What do you think? I have a buddy in Billings who offered to watch him if we needed."

"You can take him in the air?" Kristin looked surprised.

"Oh, he loves it," Casper said, reaching back and giving the dog a good scratch. Grover wagged his tail wildly, as if he knew he had just been selected for the flight. "He's been going with me since he was just a few months old. He even has a special set of goggles and ear protection. I had to rig it up for him, but he knows when he is wearing his gear it's work time."

"He sounds like a great copilot," she said as he pulled onto the road and started back toward the helo pad at the training area.

She loved on Grover, cooing into the pup's ears, and Grover ate it up as they made their way into the mountains. She was so focused on the dog that Casper wondered if she was doing her best to ignore him and what had happened.

If she didn't want to talk about it, he didn't, either. He'd just have to accept she had allowed her ex to come between them, so much so that she didn't even come to his room after she had gotten off the phone. In the end, regardless of Greg's call, she had overtly shown Casper that she didn't want him.

He had been hoping all morning that as soon as she saw him, she'd have an outpouring of apologies and explanations, but he hadn't expected this pointed avoidance. It made the sting he'd endured last night burn with a renewed pain. She had shut him down, and as much as it hurt his ego, he had to admit it probably hadn't been a bad thing.

"I talked to Cindy this morning," he said, preempting the mess they were heading into. "She said the mechanics were dropped onto the location of the helo."

Kristin perked up. "That's great. Maybe we can get the bird up and working today." Then, as if a cloud had moved overhead, her face darkened and she chanced a look at him. "Then again, that would mean I would be missing out on our adventure."

Her words made him question himself.

"So you are looking forward to our flight to Billings?" He tried to control the little sensation of giddiness that threatened to take over the logical part of his brain and make him hope for things to grow between them.

"Of course. Though," she said, smiling at

him, "I've got to admit that I hope this flight goes a little bit better. Maybe less dramatic." She stuck her tongue out him as she giggled.

The little ribbing was endearing. Especially that damn giggle.

Her phone lit up and she clicked it open, sighing.

"Good news?" he said, shifting the truck as they hit the highway.

"Oh, Greg is at it again." She clicked off the phone and dumped it into her purse.

This was his opening—it would be the perfect time to bring up his feelings about her and the guy, but based on her reaction to him simply texting, he could infer some things. Yet, assuming had never done anyone any real favors when it came to potential romances.

He had to do it—he had to get some answers. "So you said you were broken up. Yes?"

Her face grew impossibly darker. "Yes."

"If you don't want to talk about your relationship with him, I respect that," he offered, slightly relieved that they could slip that subject to the back burner as she relaxed slightly. "That being said, I do need to ask you one thing."

"What is that?" she asked, but there was an edge of a growl to her tone.

"Was he ever physically abusive toward you?"

She drew deeper into her seat. "What?" She

looked out the window, making him wonder if she was thinking about the truth of their relationship. She had to still have had feelings for Greg. Moreover, she definitely didn't have feelings for him. If she did, she would be trying to fix things between them.

Rage filled him as he thought of the man. As soon as he saw the bastard, he would be missing some teeth. "So he was?"

She shook her head. "He never hit me." She paused. "Again, though, I don't even know if what we had was a *relationship*."

Even if Greg hadn't touched her, it didn't mean that he hadn't used her and left her hurting—or worse.

He loathed the bastard.

She sighed. "I hate talking about this. I know this has to be as uncomfortable for you as it is for me."

He tapped his fingers on the gearshift as he tried to control himself.

He didn't care that they had slept together—that wasn't what bothered him, not really. He'd had relationships in the past. What bothered him was the fact this asshat had not appreciated what a wonderful woman Kristin was… Here he was, struggling to find a place in her life, but fighting against the nature of reality, while Greg had had every opportunity and hadn't seized his chance.

"Just know that I am done with him. I promise," she said, reaching out for him.

He took her hand in his. "No more feelings?"

Her phone buzzed from within her purse—she took it out and looked at the screen before pitching it back.

"Him again?" he asked.

She nodded.

"So he still has some feelings for you."

She squeezed his fingers. "I don't think so. He treats me like crap—calls me names and demeans me. If he wanted me back he's going about it in all the wrong ways."

"Well, he is definitely having a meltdown, so I guess that leads me to my next question…" He paused, trying to find exactly the right words to ask the question that needed to be asked. "Would he have set us up for failure? You know…cut that hydraulic line or anything?"

"What? No. Never." She spoke the words with conviction, but the look on her face spoke to the fact that she was considering the possibility. "There's no way he would have wanted me dead."

"Are you sure? The way he's acting isn't in line with him not being a little emotionally compromised."

She put her free hand to her neck, instinctively covering her weak point. It struck him how such a simple action could speak volumes. Though she was trying to convince him Greg wasn't their enemy, that he wasn't dangerous, her body was saying something else entirely.

"We left my bird at camp. Do you think he would have messed with anything?"

The color drained from her face. "No. There's no way." She rubbed at her neck. "I really don't think he would have done anything to put me or you in danger. He isn't a great person, but just because a dude is a jerk doesn't mean he's a criminal."

He squeezed her hand, trying to reassure her and let her know that he was listening to what she was saying, and trying to believe as she did. If nothing else, but for Kristin's sake. She didn't need a that sort of person in her life.

"He has had a lot of bad things happen to him in the past," Kristin continued. "I cut him a lot of slack in our relationship, but I would hate to think he was capable of murder."

"Anyone is capable of killing if they are given the right motivations."

She shot him a questioning glance and he could tell their conversation was making her uncomfortable.

"I just mean that Greg doesn't have a lot of great qualities, is all." He tried to deflect some of the tension, which was rising between them.

"I'm not saying your taste in men is question-able, but I think you like me, so…"

"I happen to think my taste is on point." She smiled, but the action was strained. "All I'm saying, though, is that he isn't a villain."

There was dust on the road in front of them, like someone else was making their way up to the camp as well. He tried to tell himself that Kristin was right. She knew the guy way bet-ter than he did; and, if anything, his perspec-tive of the guy would be warped because of his feelings for Kristin. He was never going to like any guy whom she had been with—it was against human nature. Though, that wasn't to say he wouldn't try.

Her phone buzzed again, but this time she didn't reach into her purse and she just let it ring.

"He will need to prove to me exactly what kind of guy he is, but right now on my list, he is enemy number one."

Chapter Twelve

Even when it came to fiction, she hated love triangles, and yet Kristin had somehow found herself right at the center of the weirdest dynamic ever. All she really wanted to do was get back to Billings and her everyday life, maybe with Casper at her side, and yet, she couldn't stop thinking about Greg and what he might have done.

If she or the team of mechanics found any indication Greg may have ambushed the helo, Casper would have been correct and she would never be able to apologize enough to overcome her failure to see the truth.

Cindy was already up and running around camp, readying for the next day of training and the next track with the rest of the team. When they parked, she was digging around in the back of her state-issued pickup, going through a large black tub of gear.

"How's it going?" Casper asked as they approached the commander, Grover at their heels.

Cindy looked up at them with a semi-annoyed expression on her face. "No matter how organized I think I am, I'm always looking for something. It's starting to really piss me off." Cindy withdrew a roll of duct tape. "There." She slammed the lid back on the tub and stood up with a look of triumph on her face.

"If you needed tape," Casper said, pointing back at his pickup, "please tell me you aren't about to go out there and try to fix the bird with it."

"Real funny." Cindy waved him off. She jumped out of the back of the pickup and gave Grover some scratches. "By the way, we dropped the mechanics at your helo earlier this morning. They haven't gotten out any word, but from what your buddy was saying, it will be at least a week to get the full go-ahead to fly it all the way back to Billings."

"Greg isn't what I would call a *buddy*." He nearly snarled.

Cindy looked surprised, but just as quickly she nodded in acknowledgement, like she understood the strained relationship the two had. "I bet you want to get back to Billings soon. I'm sure you have work waiting for you, Kristin?"

Kristin looked a little surprised, but nodded. "There's always something waiting."

"I know the feeling," Cindy said, still staring down at Grover. "If you guys want to split, I can let Greg know you headed out."

"I think that would be great," Casper said. "But, let me know if you see Greg slithering around. I was hoping to ask him about something before we left."

"You got it," Cindy said, finally looking up from the pup and sending them both a smile. "I'm sure you aren't even at the point of thinking about wanting to come back over to try and redo your training, Kristin, but we really would appreciate another chance to get the public on our side."

"I will have to take it to our team, but I can probably sell the idea." She slid a look to Casper, who was smiling. "In fact, I will try to bring it up to them as soon as I get back to Billings. I can make some calls in the meantime."

"When do you think you two are going to hit the skids?" Cindy asked.

"Actually," Casper said, "we were going to go as soon as I did a once-over on the bird."

Cindy nodded, seemingly pleased that their course for public funding could self-correct so quickly. "That's great. We can schedule your return as soon as we get word on the helo."

Casper touched her shoulder, driving excitement through her.

"If you want, I will talk to the team in Billings as well. Let's get some press on the joint efforts in the meantime. Cool?"

"I'll make the call." Cindy gave them an excited smile.

Kristin couldn't help but revel in the fact that for once, they were all getting something they wanted.

The red helo was waiting for them, and Casper lifted Grover up and in—complete with doggy goggles—and then he helped her inside, her hand in his, the effect making her even more nervous than she already was for getting back into a bird. She would have liked to have been able to talk herself into thinking everything was going to be fine and that they would have no problems in the flight or otherwise, but her thoughts kept moving to Greg and his potential sabotage.

No. He isn't like that.

Casper clicked the door closed. He walked around the helo, doing his preflight check, then climbed in next to her.

"Everything okay?" she asked, her stomach clenching.

"Looks like we are a go." He gave her a thumbs-up.

She nodded, slipping on her flight helmet and readying herself to hit the air.

Everything will be okay. A knot formed in her gut at the thought of taking to the sky again. *The odds are in our favor. This flight will be fine.*

She took a deep breath and tried to control her nerves.

It will be, as long as Greg didn't sabotage this bird, too.

She had to have been right—Greg wasn't behind them going down. If he was, their lives could once again be on the line.

The blades began to spin, picking up speed.

As they took to the air, some of her nerves stayed on the ground. Once they leveled out and moved steadily east in the sky, Casper reached over and took her hand. They were both quiet, like each was waiting for the jerk and hiss of a broken hydraulic line. Yet, time passed and nothing happened.

They twisted between the mountains, watching the lush green timber turn to the budding grasses and then river bottoms complete with the white-barked birch and stoic blue herons. Moving into the rolling plains, they crossed over a herd of antelope, their tawny bodies and white bellies flashing in the sun as they streaked away from the hum of the chopper.

There was just nothing better than being

safely tucked in the air with a snoozing dog in the back. After their last flight, this was exactly what she needed—a flight to remember just how incredible her lifestyle was.

It was almost wild to think about, after their mishap, but up here in the sky she felt more in control than she did in many of her past relationships. This was her world, her happy place.

Casper squeezed her hand just a little tighter, making her wonder if he was thinking something similar.

She was glad to be here with him. Even if they couldn't have the world together years from now, at least they could have today.

The flight didn't seem like it took any time at all and the rimrocks of Billings sprung up in the distance. Part of her wanted to tell him to keep flying, to keep them up in this reprieve from reality for as long as possible, but she also had a job to do.

They touched down on the helo pad, and he let go of her hand as she unfastened her belts. Stepping out of the helo, the euphoria she felt while they were in the air drifted from her like it too wished to be back in the sky.

Casper walked around and smiled at her as he stuck his flight helmet under his arm, Grover prancing at his side. He looked like some hero out of a Hollywood blockbuster—how had she gotten so lucky not only to befriend this man, but also to get the opportunity to kiss him? If given the chance, there was no way she could not make love to him…at least for the sake of memories.

"That went a hell of a lot better than I anticipated." Casper stretched, his T-shirt pulling tight over the curved muscles of his pecs.

How hadn't she noticed how muscular he was before? Or how he had almost a perfect six-pack that was just a little bit hidden by that low patch of hair pressing against his shirt?

If she wouldn't have felt like it was out of place here at the aviation center, she would have moved to him and made him want her just as badly as she wanted him. What she would have given to take him into a dark corner and show him what kind of an effect he had on her body.

"You okay?" Casper asked. "You look upset."

She nodded awkwardly. "Yeah… I'm fine. Just fine."

After taking care of the helo, they made their way to the parking lot with the excited Grover in tow. She texted away, working to set up a meeting with the SAR chief and coordinators in her county. As it stood, they probably wanted to meet with her to talk about the events of the weekend as well. While she wasn't in a hurry to explain the problems, and where and how things may have possibly gone wrong, she wanted to get ahead of things as much as possible. It was always better to head off problems rather than let them fester and grow.

Her phone pinged. "We have a meeting tomorrow with my team to go over the accident. I'm going to sell them on the idea of further training. No worries."

Casper nodded, but was surprisingly quiet.

"Is everything okay with you?" she asked. Oddly, an old saying came to mind—"when someone points their finger at you, three fingers point at the speaker."

He shrugged as they made their way out into the parking lot, toward her Durango.

"You know that response is going to keep me asking questions." She bumped into him playfully.

He sent her a tired smile and gave Grover a scratch. "You are going to think I'm a wimp if I admit it."

Her empathy spiked and she wanted to take him in her arms like she was his protector. "There's nothing you can't tell me."

As they stopped by her SUV, he helped Grover climb in the back seat and then stared at her. "Why do I feel like I could actually tell you anything and you wouldn't judge me?"

Touching his arm, she met his gaze. "It's because you can. We are two parts of a single soul." She smiled. "No matter what, I'm a safe place for you. You can say anything you want and it won't leave my lips. You can cry and wail and cuss, and I won't think you less of a man."

He shook his head like he didn't believe her. "That... *Why?* Why would you do something so genuinely kind for me?"

"It may sound naive, but I feel like I could do the same with you. I think it is rare in this world when two souls like ours meet. If we can't trust each other, then there is no one in this world we can."

He reached his arm around her, pulled her into him and kissed her. The motion was hungry and full of want, echoing the yearning she felt. He took hold of her face with both hands, gently stroking the soft hairs near her cheek, until she felt a heady mix of comfort and lust. When he broke from their kiss, she moved forward for more, but found him looking upon her like she was the most beautiful woman in the world.

"Let's go back to my place," she said, breathless from the power of his desire.

"Yes. Let's." He opened her door for her, grabbing her butt as she stepped up into the driver's seat.

As he moved away, she wondered if he could

feel the heat of her core as his hand had played with her ass. He had to have.

He got in, and as he did, her phone pinged with a message. Then another and another, as it buzzed and rang.

"Uh-oh," he said, motioning for her to answer the angry beast. "You better take care of that."

She cringed, picking up her phone to answer the myriad of messages hitting it. "Oh, I can't wait."

Poring through the texts and dispatches, her heart sank.

Why, when everything was finally starting to come together and go right, did everything have to go to complete chaos?

"What happened?"

Another advisory came in. "It looks like there is a missing female, thirty-one. Was last seen by her husband at their place of residence near the Rocky Mountain College."

Casper gave a long sigh. "We have to go."

The last thing she wanted to do was give up an opportunity to finally get to see Casper naked. Every part of her wanted him. *Right. Now.*

"We can continue what we have started later. I'm not going anywhere for a while."

For a while. There were the key words, and

the reason it probably was a good idea for them to go to this call.

She nodded as her phone pinged again. The county's entire search-and-rescue team was gearing up and getting ready to be sent out.

"Text them back. Tell them they have air support if they need it. We may not have FLIR on my ride, but we can still get up there and look."

She tapped out a message to her team. "I let them know we are available. At the very least, I think we could be some more boots on the ground until they are ready to call in the big guns."

Her phone pinged several more times.

"As much as I wanted to take you back to your place, I have to tell you I love the call to arms. There is something about it—the adrenaline hit that comes with knowing we are about to go out and make a difference."

"Yeah, I know that feeling. I don't ever want to lose it. The day I do, I know that my time doing this is over." She started the car, checking her phone one more time.

"Where are we meeting the team?"

"At the bottom of a trail where a man reported she had been hiking. It's not one that many people frequent. It's steep and rocky terrain. It's very possible that she had a medical emergency, so we will need to prepare for that possibility,

I'm sure." She pulled out of the parking lot and got onto the main road.

"Do you have an ID?"

She looked at her phone again, quickly pulling up the woman's photo and identifying information, and handed it over. "Take a look."

Taking the phone, he let out an odd, strangled sound. "Oh, holy…" An expletive followed.

"What is it?" she asked, slowing down.

"That's—that's my brother's wife."

Chapter Thirteen

This couldn't be a coincidence. First, his father had gone missing in this city and now his sister-in-law? What in the hell was going on?

His brother picked up on the first ring. "Hello?"

"Why didn't you call me?"

"What?" William sounded totally confused. "Casper? Why would I call you?"

He huffed in a bitter laugh. "Your wife goes missing and you don't think that I should be on your list of people to inform? Are you kidding me?"

There was a long pause on the other end of the line.

Kristin had a surprised look on her face, but then gave him a little nod, as if encouraging him to continue down the road of the tongue-lashing.

Casper paused as a thousand thoughts and questions poured through him. "You were the one who made the report, right?"

William cleared his throat. "No. Are you done jumping down my throat? If you think I didn't want you to know about Michelle going missing, you are stupid. Yet, if you think that just because you are my brother that you would be the first person I'd call when Michelle went missing, you are a complete narcissist. You don't even live here… Which begs, how did you find out?"

Just like that, he was furious. How dare his brother come at him like that? As he opened his mouth to start unleashing his fury on William, Kristin reached over and touched his arm. Her touch had an instant calming effect, like a shot of Ativan. His brother wasn't exactly wrong— he could see where he was coming from in his argument—but he didn't need to be such a jerk about it. Then again, neither did Casper. He needed to be patient with his brother. His wife had gone missing and there was no doubt he had to be lashing out due to sheer panic and desperation.

"I'm sorry," Casper said, attempting to self-correct before things took a turn that they didn't need to take. His brother already had enough on his plate. "Do you want to tell me what happened with Michelle? I'm here in Billings, going to go out with the SAR team. I want to help."

Kristin gave him an approving pat on his

arm. He let out a long sigh as he gained control over all the feelings that he was trying to work through.

There were the sounds of voices, authoritative, strong and sounding of law enforcement, coming from somewhere in the background at William's location.

"Where are you right now? Do you want me to come get you? Do you want and to try to get out there and volunteer with the unit?" Casper's questions came out in a long string, since he wanted to get everything asked as he could hear how busy his brother must have been.

"Actually, I just got done at work and now I'm talking with my lawyer. I had an appointment I couldn't get out of. I have to go. Thanks for calling and I appreciate your help."

The line went dead.

Had his brother really just hung up on him... and for a *lawyer*?

All his warning bells went off.

Why would his brother be at a lawyer's office at this very moment? Was he trying to hide something by way of his lawyers?

He threw his phone on the dashboard and sat back in his seat as he watched the city of Billings pass by his window. They were on top of one set of the rimrocks, looking down onto the belly of the beast. There was a long stretch of pull-outs, where people could park and watch the city lights from above.

Ideally, the place would have been perfect for a 1950s-style date night, but unfortunately there were a number of rusted-out and taped-together cars that had been abandoned. On the ground, as they passed, was trash, and even as they cruised by, he could make out an assortment of drug paraphernalia.

"Do you want to talk about it?" Kristin asked, sounding unsure as to whether or not she should have said anything or just let the subject of the unusual phone call rest.

"My brother is a jerk. He's always been a jerk and he will always be a jerk."

"I could hear most of it, but did he say anything about his wife—Michelle?"

He shook his head, looking back and checking on the dog, who was sitting down nicely and staring out the windows as he made himself comfortable with another adventure.

"When we get to our location, I'm going to need to get Grover set up. He's not really a trained rescue dog, but given the circumstances, I'm not leaving him in the car and I don't want to waste time handing him off. Who knows, he may surprise us."

She smiled. "I'm sure he will be an asset. I

have to tell you, he really is a good boy. I can't believe how well he did on the flight."

He was glad that he wasn't having to talk about his brother. If he did, he wasn't sure that he would have anything nice to say—even though his brother did have some almost redeemable qualities when he wasn't being a total jackass.

"Grover is my dude." At the sound of his name, Grover moved toward them, close enough that Casper could reach back and give him a good ear rub. He was lucky to have a buddy like him. He wasn't sure how he could make it through this life without his companion. It would have been unbearably lonely without him.

"Do you get along with Michelle?"

He sighed, hating to accept the fact he was going to have to face the whirlwind that was pressing down upon him and his family. "Yes, she is a nice woman. She was great about taking my dad into their home and getting caregivers for him."

"Do they have a big place?"

He motioned toward the east. "Yeah, they live on one of the bluffs on that side of town. My brother is a car salesman. Used to own a dealership, but it shuttered during the pandemic. Now, he has gone to work for a friend of his…so far as I know. Michelle was selling insurance, but I don't know much about her work."

"Did she hike a lot, do you know?"

He shrugged. "She was fit. I'm thinking she was active."

"That's a positive. If she is out there and hurt on the trail, if she is prepared for an emergency, then there is a good possibility that we can get to her and get her out pretty quickly."

"Has your team pinned her phone's location?"

"Its last location pinged at her residence."

He frowned. "That doesn't sound like her. She wouldn't go anywhere without her phone. She lives on that thing, just like the rest of the planet."

Kristin coyly slipped her phone back into the cup holder as she drove. "Maybe she wanted a break from the thing. Let's not jump to any conclusions."

"I'm not jumping to anything. All I'm thinking is that this is all just too close to what happened to my father. I mean, what are the odds that my father and now Michelle must have search-and-rescue called to find them? If she's hurt, my brother's going to have to answer to me."

"I'm sure Michelle will be fine. She is probably just out on a walk and got lost because she didn't have her phone. Time got away from her…you know the norm." Kristin tried to make him feel better. "I won't deny it's odd that your brother is on the edge of two SAR calls, but it doesn't mean that he has done anything wrong. It just means that maybe your family, and your brother specifically, are having a run of bad luck and even worse timing."

"You know I want to believe you. I want to think you are right. I just know my brother and I know he tends to do things that I wouldn't."

"Does that mean you think your brother would kill your father? Or somehow be involved in his wife's going missing?"

When she put it in those words, so simply and yet so incredibly stark, he couldn't say that he thought his brother was capable of being *evil*.

"You're right. Sometimes, and maybe this is all my years dealing with the worst of the worst, I make assumptions. Right or wrong, they have gotten me out of some tough situations." He picked up his phone again. "It's just that action is better than inaction. I guess I just want to blame what happened to my father on someone. I should have been there to take care of him more."

"You know that I can understand that. It always hurts to lose someone you love and it hurts a thousand times more when you feel like you were somehow responsible."

Her words made him think of his brother's refusal to come in and volunteer in helping to search for Michelle—though, in all reality, he wasn't really supposed to be on scene in the event she was found deceased. Normally, family members were kept at bay.

When they arrived on scene it was much like his own unit. The Billings team was setting up the command trailer at the base of the trail and there was a flurry of activity. For a while, he and Grover followed behind Kristin, tagging along as she made introductions within the small group of people. It was fun watching the activity from the perspective of an outsider, if nothing else than to see where he and his team could learn by their examples of what to do. Most people he met were friendly and nice, welcoming him in and shaking his hand. Of course, everyone loved Grover, and it made it easier to ingratiate himself to this other team.

A black Suburban pulled up to the area, and as it did, there was a slight shift in the mood. Smiles disappeared and a seriousness took over as a middle-aged man stepped out. His face had the deep wrinkles and dark eyes of a guy who had seen more death and pain than any single person should have to endure—Casper knew that look all too well. Sometimes he worried he would become like this man—marred by the trauma of his life.

"Hey, guys," the man said, his voice as rough as the man it belonged to. He made his way toward them and the nine other people in the group moved together into a circle around him.

Kristin leaned over to him and whispered, "That's our director, Roger Bell."

Even if she hadn't told him that he was the one in control of the scene, he wouldn't have questioned it. Maybe one day, if he carried on for a search-and-rescue team, he could behave like this man—in command and carrying an air of authority. It was something to see a person who was so well-respected that without even saying a word, he could be in power.

In his days in the army, he had seen people with more stars than this man, and they hadn't garnered such a response.

"First of all, let me start off by saying that I'm glad you could all make it today," Roger said, standing at the center of the group. "I know you have a lot going on in your personal lives and jobs, but we appreciate you being out here. It's my goal that we find Michelle swiftly and with as little fanfare as possible. I have been informed that media outlets are monitoring the situation, and as such, I want to remind everyone not to post or share anything on social media or with family and friends."

Already, he liked the man.

Roger looked over at him and gave him an acknowledging dip of the head. "I'm sure most of you have met our guest here today, but in case you haven't I want to introduce Casper to the group. He's a pilot out of Big Sky, near Yellowstone Park. As I'm sure most of you have heard by now, he was in an incident involving our bird."

Casper's stomach dropped. He hadn't expected the man would know who he was, let alone out him as the pilot who'd cost them their helo.

"I want to extend my thanks to you, Casper. Without your superior flying skills and knowledge, one of the greatest members of our team would have likely lost her life."

"As much as I appreciate the acknowledgement, sir," Casper said, "I feel as if I need to clear the record. All I did was my job."

The man nodded in appreciation. "And he's humble." He offered his hand and Casper took it, giving it a shake.

The group around him muttered their thanks and as he stepped back, the man closest to him slapped him on the shoulder. The woman next to Kristin leaned in and whispered something he couldn't make out, but a smile erupted on Kristin's features.

"Cute dog, by the way," Roger said, putting out his hand. Grover walked over and sniffed the man before coming back to Casper. "Kristin let me know that this case is involving your sister-in-law, and as such, I'm concerned for your welfare in this search."

Before the man could continue, Casper put up his hand and waved him to stop. "Sir, while I appreciate your concern for my well-being, I can assure you that and I am practiced in search-and-rescue and all that it may imply. Though Michelle is my sister-in-law, my relationship with her will not impact my ability to do my job."

As soon as he finished speaking, Casper questioned himself. While he had done a great deal of recoveries and lifesaving operations, it was an entirely new thing to promise that he could keep his cool if Michelle was injured.

Chapter Fourteen

Their boots crunched on the gravel as they took to the trail looking for Michelle. Casper walked in front of her, talking to Roger. As he walked, his pants pulled tight against his ass. Watching him move was making it hard to remember what task was at hand, when all she wanted to do was reach out and squeeze.

If things went well, they would have Michelle safely returned to the city before the sun disappeared from the sky. Unfortunately, ever since she had met Casper, not much had been going their way. That didn't mean things couldn't take a turn for the better, but she hated to hold out hope.

Roger turned to face her, slowly walking backward. "I wasn't aware the guy you'd been training had such an interesting résumé," he said, motioning toward Casper.

Though she couldn't really identify why, she found herself a bit proud. Casper was her friend, but she was also grateful he was making such a good impression on Roger. It would make selling the idea of going back and redoing the training that much easier.

"He's a good dude," she said. Grover came over to her and brushed against her leg as she walked, pushing his head into her hand and forcing her to love on him. There was something about the dog nosing his way into her life that reminded her a little of Casper, but in all the right ways.

They were both painfully cute, though Grover may have had the edge.

She smiled at her thought.

"I'm going to head back to the incident command center. If you need anything, and I mean anything, let me know," Roger said, looking back at Casper as he spoke.

"We got this." Kristin took a dog treat out of her pocket and handed it to Grover. "We have the best additional team member we could hope for, so it won't be long before Michelle is back with her family." Which included Casper, and once she was back, Casper could get on his way back to Big Sky and out of her life.

Maybe she didn't want to rush this search too much, after all.

"Good luck," Roger said, letting her move by him.

Though the landscape was different, scrubby and dry compared to the timbered mountainsides of the western side of the state, as they walked, she found herself thinking about how much time she had already spent hiking through the wilderness with the man in front of her. Even in the face of chaos and mayhem, she found comfort in his presence. It was strange.

They went for about a mile before she realized that the only sounds were of them walking and nothing more. "Hey, Casper?"

He stopped. "What's up?"

"Have you seen Grover lately?" she asked, looking around them, but not seeing the tan, curly-haired dog anywhere.

"I'm sure he couldn't have gone far. He normally sticks around pretty well." Casper gave a long, shrill whistle. "Grover!" he called.

They listened, and though she expected to hear the clicking of nails on rocks and the breaking of brush as the dog came running back to them, she heard nothing.

"He never runs away." Casper whistled again.

She didn't want to point out that, right now, that didn't appear to be true. "He couldn't have gone that far. I mean, how long has it been since we saw him?"

Casper cringed. "I don't know. Ten, fifteen minutes?"

"Do you think he followed Roger back to the camp?" She took out her phone and sent Roger a quick text, asking him about the dog. "I asked. I'm sure he will get back to me soon."

"Hopefully that's all that happened. Grover can get a little preoccupied and lose track of what he is supposed to be doing sometimes."

Her phone pinged and her heart sank as she read the message. "Roger hasn't seen him. We could turn around and go back?"

"He was out in front of us. Unless he got a little lost, I'm thinking we just need to keep pressing forward. Like you said, he couldn't have gotten that far." He called the dog again, but this time she could hear the panic in his voice.

"We will find him." No man or beast who had spent any real time with Casper would want to be away from him for very long. Or maybe that was just her.

She took hold of Casper's hand, trying to console him in the only way possible. "You know, maybe he got on Michelle's scent."

He nodded, looking at the trail in front of them, but there was a terror in his eyes that she hadn't seen since they had gone down. "Yeah." He whistled loudly.

Her phone pinged again with another message from Roger. "The boss wants us to stick to the plan. He will send out a crew-wide text for everyone to keep an eye out for the dog. He will be picked up by someone from our team in no time."

She had thought losing Michelle was bad enough, but she hadn't really considered losing the dog and the impact it would have on Casper.

He started to hike faster and she struggled to keep up with his pace as they both yelled for the dog. After ten minutes, her voice had started to grow hoarse from the yelling and they paused again.

"Can you text Roger, see if anyone has a ping on Grover?" Casper asked. "I shouldn't have taken him along with us, but I swear he hasn't done this before. He's never disappeared like this. I'm getting worried that something happened to him."

She patted their entwined hands. "I'm sure that nothing happened. He probably just got on the scent of something."

"Yeah, but we haven't been here before. He's not going to know how to get himself out. If someone doesn't catch him…"

"Is he chipped?" she asked.

He nodded. "That's great if someone else finds him, but what if he fell? I've heard of dogs making mistakes and going down embankments and getting hurt. What if he has a broken leg somewhere?"

She tried to comfort him, rubbing the back of his hand with hers. "Don't freak out. Any number of things could have happened to him, but I highly doubt that he is hurt. We will find him."

She pulled out her phone, but there was nothing from anyone on her team about the dog. There were only a series of pinned locations, where people had last moved during their search for Michelle.

"It looks like there are two teams to the east and four to the west. We have lots of boots on the ground," she continued.

"No one needed this," Casper said, running his hand over his face in aggravation. "I should have left Grover with my friend."

She shook her head. "You didn't know that he was going to take off—no one did. These things happen, though, and you can't blame anyone."

"Hell, yes, I can. I can blame this completely on myself. I should have leashed him."

She couldn't argue that fact with him, and it did nothing to make her—and undoubtedly him—feel any better.

They kept calling, sometimes for Grover and other times for Michelle. According to the team's plan and the time limit that the current members were on, they were only supposed to search for another mile and then they were all to head back and trade out with the next team of volunteers. The new volunteers would be searching in the dark. If no one had found the pup by the time night fell, she had the sinking feeling Grover truly would be gone.

First, Casper had lost his father, then his sister-in-law and now even his dog. As strong as he was, she wasn't sure if he could keep himself together if things didn't start turning around for him.

Her phone pinged again. There were a series of coordinates of her teammates and another message from Roger—no dog, no Michelle.

With each second and meter that passed by, Kristin's desperation intensified and her calling grew louder. Her throat was aching now, the back feeling like with each yell she was stripping away a layer of skin, like a sacrifice to the rescue gods.

As they neared their waypoint, where they were supposed to turn around and come back, Casper's hand got sweatier in hers. Though neither spoke of the reality of their situation, he knew it as well as she did. Her phone pinged as they hit their boundary point.

She stopped, pulling him to a halt beside her. He strained against her hand as he moved to keep going, but she shook her head. "We have to follow orders, Casper."

"But...they're out there somewhere."

She nodded. "And we will find them both, but we can't put ourselves in danger."

He looked out into the scrub. "They could be anywhere."

"Exactly," she said, touching his arm. "Let's go home and come back tomorrow, when we have better equipment. Let's get the drones out here."

"Yeah, drones."

His voice was choked. "Grover! Come on, buddy! Grover!"

Her heart ached from the sound of desperation in his tone. "He will come back. Our team will find him. Until then, I won't leave your side—I promise."

Chapter Fifteen

Nothing was going his way and no matter how hard he seemed to try to keep things in line, his life seemed to unravel twice as fast. Back at the base camp, they switched out with another set of volunteers to work a new set of coordinates. Roger was busy talking to the new teams and setting them up for the next track of looking, including the search for Grover.

Casper had been upset about Michelle going missing so soon after his father's death, but with his dog nowhere to be found on top of it all, it was making him lose his damn mind. In the four years he'd owned him, Grover had never done this before. In fact, he had rarely ever even left his sight. The thought that his dog was truly gone tore at him. It just wasn't possible.

Why hadn't he just put him on a leash?

He ran his hands over his face as he tried to reconcile the reality with his self-loathing.

All they could do now was keep searching.

He turned to Kristin. "I'm going back out there. I know you need to get some rest and it's getting dark, but I can't leave. I can't stop looking."

Kristin looked exhausted, but she didn't argue. "Did you hear from your brother?"

He shook his head. "You should give him a call and let him know how the search is going. In the meantime, I'm going to make some calls to my team at FLIR and see if we can get some other equipment out here."

He nodded grimly, feeling as though they were grasping at straws.

It was strange, he had been on so many of these search missions and yet this was the first time he had ever felt so helpless...and hopeless. Maybe it was because it was his dog and it wasn't like searching for a person who could possibly call out if and when they got close, even if they were hurt. Grover, if hurt, was at the mercy of the team.

He went to his bag and withdrew a leash he had stuffed in the bottom of his gear without any real intention of using. If he got Grover back, he would be on this thing anytime they even thought about getting out of a vehicle. In perpetuity, the dog was grounded.

Taking out his phone and walking to the edge of the camp for a little privacy, he called William. Just when he thought his brother wasn't going to pick up, he answered. "Did you find her?"

"So I'm taking it that you haven't heard from her, either?" Casper asked.

William huffed.

"Don't give me that," Casper said, his patience almost nonexistent. "Are you on your way or are you still too busy with your lawyers to come out and actually look for your wife?"

"What are you talking about? Some guy, Bell… I've been talking to him, and he told me that you all had it under control. 'Our teams are on it'…and 'we won't stop until we find her'. That's what he said. Are you telling me that you guys are incompetent? That you think sending me out there is the best course of action?"

Everything his brother was saying was making sense, but he couldn't come to terms with it. "If it was my wife out there, I would be the first person working the grid and trying to find her. She needs you and you are sitting who knows where and twiddling your thumbs."

"Is this really about me, Casper? Or are you angry that I'm making you look bad, or something? I don't get why you are so upset when it's not your wife who is gone."

He stopped for a moment. What was he really mad at?

"I'm not responsible for who or what you are, and I don't care what I look like to people I don't know,"

"Then what in the hell is your problem, Casper?"

"You are not going to make this my fault."

"You're crazy," William said, huffing from the other end of the line.

"William, once and for all…" He paused, knowing what he was about to ask would piss him off and possibly draw a close to any relationship they had, but he needed to know. "Did you have anything to do with Michelle's disappearance?"

His brother made a strangled noise and the phone cut off.

Just like that, his relationship with his brother was unquestionably over.

He wanted to throw his phone and yell at the sky, but he wasn't sure if it was because of his brother, or the hundred other things he was feeling right now. Maybe he had been out of line for asking his brother if he'd had anything to do with Michelle being missing. For all he knew, she would come rolling back home any minute. Maybe she was just running late or maybe she was out with girlfriends and was pissed off and playing some kind of trick on his brother. She hadn't even been missing for thirty hours yet.

He didn't know where she came from or how long she had been there, but Kristin stepped out from behind him. "So that sounds like it maybe didn't go quite as well as you were hoping."

"You can say that again." He didn't want to ask how much she'd overheard.

She cleared her throat and lifted the black plastic case she was carrying so he could get a better look. "I got my drone. We can start there. It has a small FLIR system and it's not as good as the helo unit, but it may get us on to something. I figured it's worth a try. We can run it until we can't see anything, we run out of batteries, or we find them. No matter what, though, we aren't stopping."

He pulled her into his arms and gave her a kiss on the top of her head. "Where have you been all my life?" He spoke the words into her hair. She smelled like sweat and fresh air, and it made him appreciate her that much more.

"I've been out here, searching for you…and, lately, your family," she teased, trying to make light of the darkness in which they had found themselves.

He laughed, appreciating that she wanted to make him feel better…and was succeeding. "You think you're real funny, don't you?"

"Not funny, but I'm glad I made you smile."

She ran her free hand over his lower back. "I'm here now."

Now. The word was like a razor blade, but he tried to ignore the sharpness that only he must have felt.

"By the way," she said, stepping out of his arms after a long moment, "the team working a half mile from where we were said they heard a dog barking. They can't say for sure whether or not it was Grover, but at least we have a place where we can really start looking."

It was the first glimmer of hope he'd felt since losing his furry friend.

"Let's pop smoke," he said, and she gave him a quizzical look. "You know…let's hit the trail."

"Wait, I know we talked about going from here, but let's change up," she said, stopping him in his tracks. "Let's take my truck to the lower road. From there we can work that line. It's closer to where they think they heard him and we can run the drone from the car."

"Perfect." He kissed her hands. "You really are an incredible woman."

"Do you have your bag?"

He nodded. "It's in the rig."

She pointed at the leash that was looped around his shoulder as they walked back toward her car. "You know you don't need that to drag me around. I'll happily go with you."

It caught him by surprise that she could turn his entire mood around so rapidly and he was smiling as he got into her car.

As she started to drive, her face turned serious. "Do you think your brother would hurt his wife? Really?"

He shrugged. "I don't know. I'd like to think he wouldn't, but he isn't acting like a man who is innocent. Apathy isn't the right response from a man who lost his dad. You don't see me acting like him."

"Your father's death was an accident."

"Was it?" he countered.

She frowned. "Your father got out, got lost and succumbed to his illness. There was no evidence of foul play or neglect."

"I agree," he said, putting his hands up and instinctively distancing himself from murder. "All I'm saying is that it's strange that you found him so far from where he should have been. My brother said he snuck out, but he had gone too far for him to have walked there. Someone had to have picked him up or given him a ride."

"Do you think someone picked him up on the road? That he hitchhiked?" She was playing devil's advocate, but he didn't blame her for wanting to know more.

"Someone would have seen him if he had

been hitchhiking. Billings isn't a small town. No one would have picked him up, not when he was clearly having a mental-health crisis. Passersby would have likely called something like that in."

Kristin chewed on her lip like she was struggling to hold back her thoughts. "Unless they thought he was a transient."

"Was that how he looked when you found him?" he asked, an ache forming in his gut as he thought about how far his father had fallen from the powerful, loving and professional man he had once known.

"He was carrying a stuffed lobster with bailing twine around his neck. I wouldn't say that he looked like he was well-centered."

"So he did look like a transient. That only makes me suspect my brother more."

"I'm not saying that your feelings about your brother aren't valid. You know I've got your back—especially when it comes to your intuition—but to accuse someone of events that could be best described as negligent homicide... that's pretty damned serious."

"You're telling me." He sighed, trying to staunch the ache. "I'm not about to let anyone else know what I'm thinking, though. I'm not going to jump to anything until I have definitive proof one way or another."

She pulled to a stop a few miles from incident command center and put the car in Park. "I'm sure your brother wouldn't want anyone in your family to be harmed. I mean…on top of him being your brother, you haven't given me any reason or motive behind his wanting to hurt your loved ones."

He nodded, tapping his fingers against his thigh. "You're right."

"Now, let's work on finding them." She stepped out and grabbed the drone, then set it into flight.

There was a small screen in front of her, showing the thermal readings of the environment as it flew. He tried not to delve into his fears, but they gnawed at him. He wasn't wrong about his father being too far away to easily explain his location. Someone had to have taken him to the rims. If they had, it was feasible that they wanted him to simply disappear…or jump.

The Billings rimrocks were notorious for their use as a launching pad for those who wanted to end their lives. Yet, his father hadn't seemed suicidal at all. Maybe he had escaped from the grip of whoever had taken him out there to die. Or maybe they had experienced a change of heart and decided to leave him to the mercy of the elements.

Overhead, the drone hummed as she moved it methodically over the area. Nothing unusual appeared on the screen, but he knew she wouldn't give up. She had made Casper a promise—she wouldn't be stop searching until they found Michelle and Grover.

Yet, as she flew the UAV, Casper had a sinking feeling that they weren't any closer to finding either.

He tried to control all the feelings that swelled within him. There had been so much death, then the accident and now this… He was living under a dark cloud.

He was staring at the thermal images. "What is that?" he asked, pointing at something that was far too small to be anything of interest.

"Probably a rabbit, maybe a skunk." She smiled, but the action seemed forced.

He nodded, crestfallen.

There was barking in the distance. With the flick of the stick, she sent the drone screaming off in the direction of the noise as she looked hopefully to Casper. "Do you think that was him?" There was a light in her eyes he hadn't seen there before, and a smile blessed her lips.

"That had to have been him. It just had to." He started to move in the direction of the barking. "Grover! Is that you, buddy? Grover!" He yelled the name, his sound deep and filled with hope.

The barking changed pitch, almost matching his voice, but the sound didn't grow closer.

"That's him!" Casper exclaimed, picking up his pace and hiking faster, almost at a jog.

Hopefully, Grover wasn't hurt. If he wasn't moving toward them, there had to be a reason.

They twisted through the sagebrush that littered the hillside, careful to avoid the prickly pear and step around the yucca. For a desert landscape, it was beautiful.

"Grover!" Casper called again after a few minutes.

Once again, they heard barking, but there was no sign of the dog approaching.

She flew the drone ahead of them. "There," she said, pointing at her screen. "About a quarter mile ahead. I think we found him."

Casper stopped just long enough to glance at the picture. "Does it look like he's okay?"

"I can't say. He doesn't seem to be going anywhere. Do we have a way to get him out if he is hurt? I don't want to have to waste time coming back to the car to get a blanket or something if we need to carry him out."

She lowered the drone on the dog, pulling his thermal image in closer, but as she did, Casper noticed there was something else…something cooler.

"Casper…" she whispered his name as she

looked up at him with wide eyes. "We need to call the rest of the team."

He stared at her in the waning light. "Why?"

"Casper... I think he may be lying with a body."

Chapter Sixteen

He had known the second he heard Kristin whisper his name. He couldn't explain how or why, but he just knew Grover had found Michelle.

Grover jumped up, almost skipping as Casper approached his dog. He came running over in the beam of the flashlight, his tongue lolling out of his mouth in true Grover style.

"Where have you been, buddy? You need to listen," he said, trying to sound mad, but even he could only hear the relief in his voice.

Grover licked his hand and then turn and sped back to the woman on the ground. Her dark brown hair was whipped around her face, obscuring her features. She was wearing a long black set of leggings and a sweatshirt. Over top was a light gray down vest.

"Michelle?" he called her name in hopes that she might possibly still have been alive.

However, the thermal scan had already made

the possibility of her being alive slim to none—unless she was extremely hypothermic.

There was no response.

He was surprised, but a hollow sensation filled him as he moved toward her.

Her head was turned and she was lying on the ground, a pool of blood around her... It was Michelle.

There was the glow of red and blue lights coming toward them in the distance.

They didn't need to rush.

Grover came back to him and sat in front of his feet as though he was blocking him from going any farther, like he didn't want him to have to witness the gruesome scene before them.

Kristin stopped beside them. "Why don't you just stay here? I can take care of this."

There was no way he was ever going to let her fall on this sword. "No, let's do it together."

He took the lead and moved closer to the body. Michelle was lying on her stomach between a large yucca plant and two round sage brushes. Her head was turned at a strange angle. Not far from where she was lying was a large overhang. There was no rise and fall as she tried to breathe. There was only...*stillness* and the damn emergency vehicle lights.

Knowing what he would find, he kneeled

down and pressed his fingers against the cold flesh of the woman's neck. There was no pulse.

Though he knew he shouldn't disturb the body, he pushed back a bit of the hair that had stuck in the blood near the corner of her lips so he could make out the woman's face. What little hope he had been carrying that this may have been someone else drifted away. Without a doubt, this was the woman they had been hoping to find alive and well.

Kristin grazed the top of his shoulder in question.

"Nothing. She's gone." He stood up, rubbing his fingers against the legs of his pants, like he could somehow wipe the death from them, but what he had felt he could not unfeel.

"Are you okay?" she whispered, as if speaking loudly would somehow disturb the woman lying before them.

"Yeah," he said, his voice cracking, so he cleared his throat. "Yeah, I'm fine."

He moved the flashlight from the top of her head down to her feet. She was wearing running shoes, with dirt on the toes. Her left arm was wrenched behind her body and the ring on her finger flashed in the harsh beam of light.

He hadn't asked his brother if he and Michelle had been fighting or if anything had been off between the two of them. It was possible that

Michelle had been running in the early morning hours and not seen the steep overhang.

He flashed the light in the direction of the cliff near them. It was high up, but he wondered if it was a far enough fall to actually result in her presenting as she was. Then again, someone could fall a matter of inches, and if they hit their head just right it could result in death. The human body could be so fragile, but on the other side of the coin, could withstand so much—and that was to say nothing of a person's heart.

"Did you see any indication as to the cause of death?"

"There's blood in and around her mouth." He closed his eyes for a second and he thought about the way her lifeless eyes had been staring into the nothingness. "That could indicate a possible trauma event to the lungs. Or she could have bit her tongue. Who knows. Without moving her, it's hard to even guess."

He moved the light over her back again, looking but not seeing any obvious bullet holes or bludgeoning marks.

"If I had to guess," he said, motioning in the direction of the little cliff, "she fell. Maybe she broke some ribs and she laid there, unconscious until she died."

"I hope she went quickly."

"That's all anyone can hope for," he said, moving Kristin away from the body.

There were the sounds of voices as people moved up the hillside toward them. Even though he had yet to see them, he could make out the crackle and static of handsets of the law-enforcement officers who must have been leading the charge.

Grover came over to him and sat down, so Casper clipped the leash firmly in place, giving it a gentle tug and ensuring it wouldn't go anywhere. The dog leaned against his leg and looked up at him, giving him the biggest eyes in what he assumed was an apology.

"How do you think Grover found her?"

"Doodles have an incredible sense of smell and they have even more incredible hearts. All this dude does is love."

"And find people." She smiled, but it weighed on her.

"Yeah, and well, that. That is new talent, though." He scratched the pup. "I guess his food can be a write-off if he is an active member of the SAR team. Right?"

"I think they may start asking questions when you feed 'him'—" she did finger quotes as she teased "—filet mignon every night."

"Oh, and I'm… I mean *he's* a burger fan, too." He laughed and the sound hit a sour note as his flashlight's beam moved over the body lying near them.

Kristin reached over and started to love on Grover. "It's okay to seek a little levity in situations like these."

"Michelle was married to William—she had to have a sense of humor." He smiled. "I mean any poor woman who had to see him in the buff would have to be able to laugh."

Kristin giggled, but she clapped her hands over her mouth like she felt as off about their joking as he did.

Normally, he didn't have these kinds of issues when he was dealing with the dead. In fact, he had grown more accustomed to it than he would have liked. Before his father's death, he was known for being able to go from a body retrieval to his buddy's baby shower. The baby hadn't liked him, crying when his buddy's wife had put the little one into his arms—he'd blamed the smell, but he couldn't really blame the baby for not liking him. He'd never been much of a baby person.

Michelle and his brother had been talking about having a family for a long time. From what his brother had alluded to, they'd been having fertility issues. IVF had been outside their budget, and adoption was something Michelle hadn't wanted.

"I need to call my brother."

Kristin met his gaze in the dark. "Do you think that is the best idea?"

"Why? Don't you?"

"You are already at odds with him. If you are the one to tell him his wife has been found deceased, whatever chances you have of re-kindling your relationship with him would be gone."

"You think he would rather hear the news from a stranger?"

"Sometimes a stranger is the best person when it comes to delivering bad news."

He sighed. There was a lot riding on this decision. If his brother was somehow involved with anything to do with Michelle's death, it would be best if the police were the ones to speak to him first. He didn't want to give him a chance to be a step ahead of the investigators if he was guilty. If he was innocent of any misdeeds, as Casper hoped, he would forever think about him as the one to drive the stake of loss.

If nothing else, he needed to be careful about any legal ramifications.

"She and your brother were getting along? I know how rifts happen in relationships." Kristin shifted her weight, like the conversation was striking a little too close to home for her comfort.

"My brother doesn't open up to me."

Grover whined.

A light flashed over them as one of the officers in the front of the group of hikers came over the top of the hill and into view. He was wearing a fleece cap with a search-and-rescue patch sewn to the front. He was big and carried himself like he lifted weights more than the average guy.

"Hello, Officer," Casper said, giving the guy approaching them an awkward wave. "The body is here."

"Did you identify her as the woman we have been searching for?"

"Yes. It's my sister-in-law, Michelle Keller."

The guy gave him a wary side-eye. "Your sister-in-law? Really. Interesting."

"I'm a helo pilot from the Big Sky SAR team, I was here with—"

"Me," Kristin said, speaking up, "I'm the FLIR tech. You and I have met before, Sergeant Miller."

He moved his flashlight so he could better see her face. "Hey, Ms. Loren, sorry I didn't recognize you."

She waved him off. "It's dark. We're just glad you're here."

"You guys didn't touch anything, did you?"

Kristin shook her head.

"I moved Michelle's hair slightly so I could see if she had a pulse."

"And you both arrived on scene together?"

Casper lifted the leash slightly. "Yes, but my dog was actually the one to find her. I didn't see any evidence that my dog bothered her, but with it being as dark as it is… I can't say for sure."

Sergeant Miller nodded. "I'm glad your dog found her. This the dog we were supposed to be keeping an eye out for?"

"He self-volunteered for the search." Kristin chuckled. "Turns out he was better at finding Michelle than the rest of us. He actually barked, if he hadn't, I don't know that we would have found the body until tomorrow. Everyone was still working the primary location."

Miller walked up and patted Grover on the head. The dog gave him a lick and the guy actually smiled. The action was so fleeting and awkward that he could tell it was something the man rarely did. He felt for the guy.

The rest of the group made their way over the hill. One of the men was huffing like he had jogged to catch up. Officer Miller turned to face the three people who had followed him up. "All right, everyone, we have a death on our hands. This area is now under an active investigation. As such, please do not touch any items, or disturb the area." He turned toward the body and, as if he had to reaffirm Casper's findings, kneeled down and reached to check Michelle's pulse.

Finding none, he wiped his hands on his pants. The action was so strangely the same as his, that Casper found himself wondering if it was something that everyone inadvertently did—as if this aversion to death was part of the human condition.

Miller stood up, slipped out his phone and proceeded to take a variety of pictures around the body. The camera flashed, making orbs dance in Casper's vision as he stared out into the night. Seemingly satisfied with the photos, he tapped away on his phone. He was probably reaching out to the rest of his people so they could come out and help him investigate the scene.

If things went well and they determined Michelle's death had been nothing more than a tragic accident, they would have her off to the medical examiner by dawn. If not, it would take longer, as they would have to get the on-call detective out here to go over the scene and pull together all the information for a more thorough investigation. If that was the case, he and his brother would be in trouble.

It would look strange to the detectives when he told them about the phone call with his brother and his meeting with the attorney. And, while it was explainable, Casper's being here was a little strange. This was all to say nothing about the fact of his father's recent death and search to find him.

There was such a thing as a string of bad luck, but in cases like these, nefarious deeds and family drama were far more common.

Kristin had moved toward the group of on-lookers and he recognized the man she was speaking to as Roger Bell. He looked exhausted, but maybe the thin light of the flashlights was doing him no favors.

Roger caught him looking and waved him over toward them, and he obliged.

"So sorry to see things go this way, Keller."

Casper gave him an acknowledging tip of the head. "'Preciate that. I was hoping we would find her, unharmed."

"As we all were." Roger gave him a bump to the shoulder. "You know—" Roger looked to Kristin "—you both went against orders in coming out here, to this area. You were supposed to be having your legally required break. That's not our policy or procedure and, you know, if lawyers get a hold of it…it could affect the ruling if there is any kind of criminal case."

Kristin frowned. "I'm aware, sir, but given the circumstances—this being a member of his family and his dog that were missing—there was no way we could walk away."

"I understand that, but you shouldn't have gone out here without letting your superiors know." He turned to him. "Aren't you one of the more important members of your team in Big Sky?"

"Just a regular member," Casper said, not wanting to add the fact that his role after the crash was tenuous. The only thing, or person, keeping him safely in his job was Cindy.

"Regardless, you both knew better. I am grateful that you all found Michelle and we can let the family know the search is over, but we are going to have to revisit both of your blatant disregard for procedures."

Casper wasn't worried about Roger calling Cindy and voicing a complaint. There were always standard time limits for SAR members to work, but as far as Casper knew, there were no policies in place in his unit that talked about a private citizen working an area outside the immediate search area. If there was one, he doubted he could be let go from the unit Though, if anyone else besides Cindy got the call, there might be slightly more fireworks.

The same couldn't be said of Kristin.

"You shouldn't be condemning her for her actions. She wasn't the one on point here. I was the one who made her come along so I wouldn't be searching alone. You should commend her for wanting to keep an outsider safe."

"Keeping you safe wasn't her job. Her job was to listen to orders. In fact, as a FLIR tech, she is lucky that I even allowed her to be out here on scene—especially given the latest drama with her and her aviation team. She's already given me enough headaches. I didn't need this one on top of them all."

Though the man was officially following protocol, he was annoyed. There was enough gray area in their line of work that the man could have turned a blind eye.

"Look, Roger…" Casper said, trying to remain calm though he wanted to tell the man to take his reprimand and stick it where the sun didn't shine. "You have every right to be upset with all the events of the week, but none of the events, and I mean *none* of them, were her fault."

"Casper, need I remind you that you are here by invitation only?" Roger said, fire in his eyes. "As such, you and your friend here are relieved of duty."

Chapter Seventeen

Just like that, Kristin was sent home. When she went back to FLIR Tech, she would have a lot of explaining to do. She'd already had enough without being handed her hat for one of the tech business's best partnerships.

They made the drive back to her place in silence, which she appreciated. She didn't bother to ask him if he wanted to stay with her and he didn't bring it up. Him sleeping alone in some hotel wasn't an option. They both needed company tonight.

She wasn't anticipating sex, no. What she really wanted, and needed, was to know that there was another soul in this world who desired her, who wanted to be close. That's it. If she wasn't needed and living for others, she was without purpose. Though it wasn't healthy to see life like this, she didn't care right now—self-pity needed to happen. Or, was it self-care in taking as long as it took to look into herself and accept attention, and perhaps affection, from someone who cared for her?

If he left in the morning and went back to Big Sky, it called into question whether bringing him to her home was really the best idea. If they ended up in bed together, it was arguably self-sabotage. Yes, it would feel great to have him for the night, but it would only leave her more broken in the morning.

Before pulling down her street, she considered turning left and running back toward the city center and the DoubleTree.

She tapped her hands on the steering wheel like some attempt at Morse code to the universe, begging for it to answer. Instead of the universe, Casper reached over and took her hand, lacing their fingers together in solidarity.

"It's been a long day. Don't overthink this." He smiled and his eyes looked as tired as her heart. "You are safe with me."

In those simple words, she felt the truth, and it was freeing.

He truly was an incredible man.

"You don't know how much I needed to hear you say that." She pressed their hands to her face and he gently stroked her cheek before they dropped their hands down to the console and let the silence take over once again.

She parked in her garage, and the place was

nearly empty except for a few plastic bins, some normal maintenance tools and an unplugged extra fridge the former owner had left behind. It was strange, but she'd never really paid attention to how devoid her garage was of her personality—or maybe it personified it.

She released an audible groan.

"What's wrong?" he asked, looking almost afraid that she was going to say something that would hurt him, making her realize he was feeling just as vulnerable.

"Oh, don't worry. I was just thinking about how pathetic my place is. It's pretty minimalist."

"All I need is a blanket and a spot for the pup, and even the blanket is negotiable."

"Isn't everything?" she teased.

"Truth," he said with a little smile.

"I can do better than a blanket. If Grover needs his own bedroom, like your place, we can figure something out, but it may include you and I sleeping together." Her statement made her blush. She hadn't intended to make it sound so *dirty* and yet, she didn't regret saying something.

"If the offer is on the table," he said with a huge grin.

"Well, it's not on the table, but I guess it could be there, too, if you wanted."

"Oh, Kris, I like you talking like that."

"What did you think? I was just some plain Jane? I'm a goddess when it comes to pleasing and being pleased."

He leaned over and kissed her, the action so powerful and hungry that her entire body throbbed with want. Reaching over, he took her face in his hands and pulled back slightly, just so he could look her in the eyes. "I know you are playing," he said, his voice raspy with lust, "and if you don't want to take things any further than this, I promise it'll end here. I told you that you were safe with me, and I meant it. I'm not going to push you for something you are not ready to give."

Right now, he could have asked her to give anything and she probably would have done it just to have him in her bed. However, she appreciated that one of them was still using their right brain. They didn't need to bring sex into their relationship. If they didn't, they could keep on holding hands and being safely attracted to one another without the additional complications that came with spending a night in the other's arms.

"Let's just go and get Grover settled. I'd say we could have a glass of wine or a beer or something, but as things are, I think it would be best if we both came to our decisions with a clear head. If we take things further, I don't want you to regret anything, and neither do I."

He let go of her hand, but he looked lighter. "I have to say it is nice being with a real adult. You know…someone who thinks things through instead of just jumping into bad decisions."

"So you think that taking things further would be a bad decision?" She frowned.

He put his hand to the car's door handle like he was looking for a quick escape. "That's not what I was saying. I didn't mean for it to come out like that. I guess what I should have said was that it's nice to have someone who is self-aware and wants to make choices that are the best for everyone involved."

She wasn't sure that his second attempt in reassuring her their sleeping together wasn't a bad idea was any better than the first, but she didn't want any more clarification. He was on the fence about the idea of being intimate just as much as she was—and that was enough to take it off the metaphorical table.

Grover led the way into the house, and the smell of trapped air and vanilla candles filled the space. It was strange how one open door could make something go from stale to re-freshed in just a few moments. Maybe she was like this place—used to her safety and her routines and comfortable with her doors closed, but needing to push that one part of her life open so she could refresh her soul.

Ugh. She hated self-reflections. It was just so much easier to constantly work, to face the needs of the day instead of the needs of her being.

Grover led her straight to the kitchen.

"Are you hungry, buddy?" She went to the fridge, knowing before she even opened it that it was about as barren as her garage. "Are you hungry, Casper?"

It had been several hours since they had eaten last and as she stood with the dog, she couldn't ignore the growling deep in her belly.

Casper walked up behind her and put his hand gently on her back as she leaned down and stared at the lonely block of cheese, eggs and some bacon still in its wrapper.

She looked over her shoulder at him. "I have enough to whip together a little breakfast for supper."

"Did you just say *supper*?" He chuckled. "My grandmother used to say that all the time."

"Are you saying I remind you of your grandmother?"

He really hadn't been earning any points in the last few minutes.

A faint redness moved into his cheeks. "Damn it. No, that's not what I meant, at all. I was just… *Gah.*" He ran his hands over his face like he could rub away his embarrassment. "It was a compliment, I swear."

"Uh-huh," she said, reaching into the fridge and taking out the ingredients she needed.

"Seriously, why am I suddenly acting like such an idiot?"

"I must be making you uncomfortable, but you don't need to be." She touched his arm as she moved by him, trying to put him at ease.

He tensed under her touch as though she was what was making him uncomfortable, not the situation. She could understand the situation, but he had been the one to make the move in the car…and pretty much every move before so it made no sense to her that he would be ill-at-ease with her fingers.

Nothing was going as she had hoped…not that she'd had any expectations.

She moved by him. "Here, open up the bacon. There is a pan by the stove there," she said, pointing toward the white shaker-style cupboard beside the range. "You good in the kitchen?"

Even though there had been nothing provocative about what she said, she couldn't help but hear it in her words. What was wrong with her?

Lust. Lust was what was wrong with her.

She was losing her ever-loving mind.

The world always said men weren't that complicated. This was a lie and whoever had made that universal assumption was an ass. Men were just as complicated as women, even if no one wanted to admit or talk about the reality that no one was different when it came to navigating emotional and relationship minefields—only the naive ventured, unafraid.

Grover lay down at the mouth of the kitchen, watching them work and do the dance of cooking. They moved almost in tandem, like they had done this kind of thing a thousand times before. She found a beauty in the dance, a familiarity that came with him even when few words were spoken.

She couldn't remember the last time she had felt something like that, and she was met with a blade of sadness that he didn't feel this same level of comfort in her home—and yet, as they worked some of the awkwardness seemed to slip away from him.

The bacon started to sizzle and they stood there, watching the meat shrink in the pan as it gave off its delicious aroma. Her mouth watered.

He moved behind her and wrapped his arms around her waist. His mouth moved against the back of her head and she could feel some of her hairs stick to the moisture on his lips. He reached up and flipped away the offending hair.

"I'm sorry for being weird." He pulled her

gently against him and she let her body relax into his.

"It's okay. Ours is a strange world and there isn't a road map for where we've been or where we might want to go."

"Where is it that you want to go?" He asked the question into her hair.

She was glad she wasn't facing him so he couldn't see the tug-of-war of emotions playing out on her features. "Casper, to be honest… I don't know."

It felt strange speaking her truth, but at the same time she was proud of herself. In so many relationships of her past, she had been afraid to be direct with her needs.

"What do you mean?"

"We both know that the elephant in the room, aside from Grover," she said, trying to joke a bit to try and alleviate some of the tension, "is that there is a big distance between you and me. If we are going to try and have a relationship there are going to be a lot of windshield hours. We are both old enough and experienced enough to know how that kind of thing usually works out. I've had relationships fail even when we were in the same city because there was a lack of time."

Her mind wandered to asking him if he was interested in moving, if they were together. He had mentioned that he was a freelancer and retired from the military, but he owned a home and was settled in his life in Big Sky. Besides, they had just met. She wasn't completely sold he wanted to spend the night with her in the same bed, let alone move hours away from his home just so they could go out on regular dates.

He slowly chewed a piece of bacon he had popped in his mouth and was staring down at the pan like it held all the answers. "I think if you wanted to try, I'd be game to seeing if we could give it a go for a bit." He looked over at her and his eyes were wide with what she could best describe as insecurity and fear.

Did he really think she would turn an offer to date him—*really* date him—down?

She hated to think of Greg at a time like this, but what Casper had just offered was more than nearly any promises Greg had made. In fact, she couldn't remember the last time a guy had wanted anything from her besides a meal and a night in the sack.

Wait...that's what we're doing now. She smirked at her thought. *This is different.*

"You want to try?" He stood up and pulled her into his arms, and looped his hands around her hips. His hands fell to her ass, but all she really noticed was the way he was looking at her.

He wanted her. Not just for tonight.

"You know I want to, Casper."

It wasn't love. It wasn't promises. It wasn't forever. However, it gave her something she hadn't felt in a long time—hope for a better life.

She turned off the stove, then moved the pans onto the back burners and covered them up so the food wouldn't dry.

"I know I promised to feed you, but I want something else right now."

"Oh?" He gave her a knowing but sly grin. "What is it that you want?"

She pressed her body harder against him. "If you have to ask that question, maybe I shouldn't—"

He cut off her words with a kiss. It was deep, hungry with want. He tasted like bacon and salt, and she savored the flavor of his lips, licking and nibbling as they gave in to their desire for each other.

Oh, to be kissed like this.

She wrapped her arms around him, reached up and pressed her fingers into his hair, pulling him harder against her lips until their tongues met. He kissed her, slowly but wild and free, pressing and holding, tracing her lips and moving deep. If his kiss was any indication of what he would be like in bed, she was a lucky woman.

Hell, she was already a lucky woman for finding herself standing here in her kitchen with the most handsome man she had ever laid eyes upon and a man who wanted something more than a one-night stand.

"Kristin…" He spoke her name into her open mouth, like he wanted her to swallow the sweet sound. "I want you."

She took him by the hand and led him a few steps into the open living room and the large couch at its center. After letting go of him, she grabbed the remote for the TV and turned on a 90s hits channel.

"Sit," she ordered, pointing at the chaise lounge section.

"Yes, ma'am." He had a huge grin on his face and his eyes were bright. "What is happening here?"

She reached up and slowly unbuttoned her shirt, moving her body with the rhythm of Def Leppard's "Pour Some Sugar on Me." This song had been around longer than her, but anytime she heard it, she had always imagined a moment like this, stripping for a man who waited to ravish her body.

Her fingers trembled with excitement as she undid her last button and slipped the cotton shirt from her shoulders, exposing her black lace bra. She would have been lying if she didn't admit that she had been imagining the day would lead here when she'd dressed. Better, she had even shaved and had an everything-gets-exfoliated-and-buffed shower.

She unzipped her jeans and pushed them down her thighs, trying in vain to keep with the music, but realizing that she was not equipped or lithe enough to make stripping her career. Thankfully, he didn't laugh at her or seem to be anything but intoxicated by her best attempt to be sexy.

She stood up and moved closer to him and he ran his fingers over the smooth skin of her lower belly, just above her panty line. She sucked in her breath as he reached around and took her ass into his hands and pulled her against his mouth. He kissed her over her panties like he had kissed her mouth, his tongue flicking against her.

A moan escaped her lips as he let go of her with one hand and moved her panties to the side so he could slip his fingers into her wet center.

"Casper..." She exhaled his name as he found the spot at her core... "Yes. Right there."

He worked her harder, faster, running the tips of his fingers over the sweet spot and licking her through the lace. As good as her fantasies about him had been, the reality of feeling him inside and on her were so much sweeter.

Her legs started to quiver and shake as he worked with the pace of her breathing. She edged to the moment, so close. Her release was right there, but she stopped, wanting the pain and ache of the climax to prolong. "I want you inside me."

Though she wasn't sure he'd heard her, she pulled down her panties and he unzipped his pants. He moved them just far enough down his thighs to not be painful, but no more than necessary as she moved on top of him. He was larger than she had expected, and she groaned as he pressed into her.

Moving her hips to the cadence of his body, it didn't take long for her to know this man was everything she had been hoping to find. He filled her to the point of nearing glorious, blissful pain, the kind that made her want to tip back her head and howl like a primal animal in the deepest recesses of pleasure.

He was hers.

She was his.

And, damn it, did he know how to pleasure her.

Every inch of him fit her as if he'd been made especially for her body. His tip pressed upward, hitting parts of her that she didn't even know existed. He rubbed against her, harder and faster, until she could feel the pressing need to release.

"You… I'm going to…" she panted as he moved faster.

She couldn't hold back. A howl escaped her…and she was free.

Chapter Eighteen

There were a handful of nights in his life that he would have given anything to go back and re-live, and last night had been one of them. When Kristin had fallen asleep in his arms, he had tried not to stare at her perfect, round-tipped nose, or the way her eyebrows arched like bows over her long black eyelashes. She'd hummed lightly in her sleep, like she was singing to the night and to him, and it had made him fall for her that much more.

After letting Grover out and getting him comfortable in her place, they had taken off to work for the day. As she drove toward his brother's house, he watched as the morning sun danced on her hair and caressed her face in the places where his fingers and touched her skin last night. Oh, he would need to make love to her again and again...and again.

There was no way he could ever grow weary in making love to her. Everything was the best—maybe it was the passion that burned between them and the lust for each other, or maybe it was that they were both just *in*, but whatever it was no one had ever made him feel as she had.

The future was written on everything about her.

She looked at him and caught him staring at her. "You okay over there? Nervous about seeing your brother?"

He shook his head. If she hadn't spoken up, he would have probably stayed in his happy place, looking at her until he had completely lost track of what they were intending on doing today.

"Did you text him to let him know we are on the way?"

"I'm not sure if I told him we were coming that he would open the door." He wished he was kidding.

"Roger said that he had been notified about Michelle's death. I think the officer may have asked him a few questions, but I don't know if they are going to look at him as a suspect in her death, or not."

"Did Roger say if they had any more idea as to the cause of death?"

She tapped her fingers on the wheel. "Nothing conclusive, but they found some interesting evidence this morning. He didn't tell me what, but I think they are leaning toward her death being a homicide."

The ache in his gut, the one that had been there since he'd found out about her being missing but had forgotten about in the night, returned, tighter than ever. He couldn't say why, other than his brother being at the lawyer's yesterday, but he had a feeling William was somehow involved and he hated it.

He hoped that he was wrong and his brother was an innocent man, but until he looked into his eyes and asked him to tell him the truth, he couldn't be sure.

"I'm impressed that you have been talking to Roger, at all." He hadn't wanted to bring it up, but since she was talking about him, he had to say something.

"He was upset last night. I'm hoping that with a little buttering up he will come to his senses and see that, if we did somehow step out of line and not follow a policy, it is the policy that is wrong and not us."

He wished he could agree with her, but he could understand why her commander would be upset with them not listening to orders and skirting his authority. In the military, nothing like that—no matter how well-intentioned—would have been considered acceptable. A person was to do as ordered.

When he'd been active, he'd been the kind who followed orders well. Toward the end of his career, though, he'd been the one giving them— and maybe that was why he had been okay in coloring outside the lines a bit last night.

His brother was outside, watering freshly planted flowers in the small garden in front of his and Michelle's house. The last time he had been there was Thanksgiving, and at the time the house had been warm and inviting. His father had been alive then, living in their basement apartment, and all in all, the holiday had been tense, but nice.

Michelle had been very inviting.

Damn. That was the last time I saw her alive.

He blinked and the image of her dead body flashed to the front of his mind. He could clearly make out the hair covering her face. He hadn't noticed it yesterday, but as he thought about the scene, he could recall the strong smell of sagebrush and something else…something chemical.

His mind must have been playing tricks on him. Maybe he was planting false memories or something just because Roger had mentioned they'd found some *interesting* things on the scene. Maybe now Casper was trying to remember all the things he might have missed.

He couldn't go there. No doubt there were high-caliber detectives on the case who were paid to go down the what-if and whodunit rabbit hole. His job was to support his family and be there for his brother in his time of need—no more, no less.

If someone had murdered Michelle, he couldn't help but wonder if they had also played some kind of role in his father's death as well. Although the official cause of death was a heart attack, it had been brought on by exposure to the elements. If someone had dumped him, he was sure that a good attorney would at least go for a charge of negligent homicide.

His brother looked up as they approached and pulled to a stop in front of the house. When William spotted them, Casper saw the passive look of a man tending to his garden was quickly replaced by one of surprise.

He half expected his brother to turn and head into the house, locking the door, and them, out of his life. Instead, William walked out toward the Durango and waited for them to step out of the car.

"I'm glad you're here. I didn't think you'd come."

His brother's warmth was in direct opposition to the coldness he felt after yesterday's conversation.

"Are you doing okay?"

William opened his mouth to speak, but

looked as though he'd choked up and swallowed his feelings down.

Giving him a moment to regain his composure, he motioned toward Kristin, who was standing at the front of the car, her hands folded in front of her like she was deeply uncomfortable being here. Maybe he had made a mistake in having her come along. "This is Kristin. She was one of the volunteers who helped find Michelle…and Dad."

William reached out, took her hand in his and looked her in the eyes. "I can't tell you how grateful I am for your help. I'm sorry I couldn't be there when you found Michelle." As he spoke, there was a crack of emotions.

As genuine as his brother seemed to be, it came off to Casper as cloying at best. His brother had never really been the emotional type. Maybe it was just his brotherly animosity that was pulling him in so many directions and kept him wanting to be mad at his brother, or maybe his intuition was trying to pull him in the right direction.

As much as he told people that they had to trust their gut, his feelings for his brother were so in flux that he couldn't rightly condemn him for a crime or crimes he may not have committed, no matter how badly he wanted to continue to point the finger.

He had to quell his annoyance. Emotions were good. In fact, in this situation, they should have been expected—if it had been anyone else, he would have. It probably didn't help that his brother was touching Kristin.

Stomp the anger down, he reminded himself.

"It was a good thing you weren't there." Casper pointed to the door. "Why don't we go inside and we can talk without your entire neighborhood being in the know."

His brother nodded, letting go of Kristin's hand, much to Casper's relief. "Yeah, I think I have a beer in the fridge or something."

Casper looked at his watch. "Bro, it's nine in the morning." Kristin shot him a look of admonishment. "But, hey, if you need to tie one on to get through the day, I get it."

Kristin gave him an almost imperceptible nod.

"Yeah. I don't really know what I need right now." His brother turned and went to the front door. As he walked, Casper noticed that his shorts were torn up and dirty in the back, and they reminded him of the state his father had been in when they found him on the rimrocks. The majority of his feelings of annoyance slipped from him.

His brother was hurting.

In all reality, so was Casper. And seeing his

brother in such a state made everything that was happening so…*permanent*. Up until now, he'd been in what he could have best described as a stunned trance. He had liked Michelle, he had been sad when they found her, he had thoughts and memories of her and their family, but he hadn't been forced to see the hole she had left behind. Losing her was compounding his brother's grief in ways he hadn't imagined.

When they walked into his brother's house, the smell of rotting garbage filled his nostrils. There were open food containers sitting on the living room table, stacked and buzzing with flies—a far cry from the last time he'd been here. Every other time he had ever been to the house, it had been picture perfect to the point it could have been in a magazine or something.

"How long was Michelle gone?" he asked, walking past his brother toward the kitchen.

"She—she left right after Dad." William threw himself down on the couch, not seeming to notice the chaos or the group of flies that took flight as he flopped.

"Two weeks?" Kristin asked, looking around like she could tell just as Casper could have easily been months and not simply weeks based on the disarray.

"Well, we have been working on things ever since Christmas. She didn't officially move out until Dad passed, but she really hadn't been living here for months."

"Did you think she may have had the intention to return home at some point?"

"I wanted her to come back. I've been calling her all the time, trying to get her to see reason. She knows I needed her. Dad's death was really hard on me." William dropped his head into his hands.

"Do you know where she had been staying?"

"I am not sure, but I think she was staying with another guy. It would take her hours to drive back—so maybe on the other side of the state. Who knows, though. She wasn't telling me anything."

Casper opened up the kitchen pantry, grabbed a large black garbage bag and started to pick up the empty beer and wine bottles that were littered all over the kitchen counter, some tipped over and having spilled their contents onto the surface, where they had been left so long that there were only purple and tan sticky globs.

Even in college, his brother hadn't been this bad off. If anything, he'd been a meticulous neat freak. He'd even made a point, regardless of his girlfriend status, to change out his bedsheets every four days. Clothes never sat in the washer and dryer—he'd even folded Casper's and put them on the bed when he'd been too busy to get to them before William had needed the washer. Casper may have depended on his brother cleaning up behind him on more than one occasion, and, of course, William had done so without much complaint.

On the corner of the counter, next to the empty coffee maker, was a huge stack of orange-and-white pill bottles with his father's name on them. There must have been at least forty different bottles. He recognized a few as normal heart meds and the like, but others he couldn't have named if he had a gun to his head. They looked rather untouched in comparison to the rest of the house and he found a strange comfort in the thought.

He filled the first bag and grabbed another, handing it to William. "I know you probably don't want to hear this, but the best thing we can do is to get you moving. Looking at the state of this place, well…you should have called me and told me what was happening with you."

"You were already pissed off," William countered, correctly. "I've been working from home and everything would have been fine, but then…" He choked up and rubbed the back of his hand hard under his nose.

Kristin was shaking her head at him, like she didn't agree with his method for helping. He didn't know if it was the right thing, either, but he couldn't just let his brother sink further into self-pity and pain.

"Come on. Get up," Casper said, wishing he had been more patient with his brother. He had just never seen him behave like this. It was so out of character, but so was losing most of the people a person loved in a short span of time.

He held out his hand, pulling his brother to standing. Kristin walked to the kitchen and started unloading the dishwasher. Casper had William hold the garbage bag and he threw more refuse into the thing.

It didn't take them long to have the place back to a livable standard. Kristin had started to vacuum, and the sounds of crumbs and detritus whipping through the tube filled the air.

After throwing six bags of trash out into the dumpster, he made William follow him upstairs to the bedroom. It was almost as bad as the living room, but instead of food boxes, there were layers upon layers of dirty clothing. The closet had just a smattering of empty hangers, except one, which had a suit jacket hanging precariously from it.

He couldn't leave his brother like this, in this state. Even if they got it all cleaned up and looking okay, his brother was not in a place where Casper could trust him to be alone. Especially after last night. Though he still couldn't say with one-hundred-percent certainty that his brother had a role in Michelle's death, he could at least say that he doubted his brother could have, or would have, left his house to commit the crime.

He started to pull the sheets from the bed after grabbing handfuls of clothing and throwing them into the center of the bed, making a makeshift laundry roll. "Didn't you say you had a meeting with your lawyer yesterday?"

William nodded.

"Did you go to their office?"

"It was online. Talked to the mediator, mostly."

"What were you talking to the lawyer about?"

"Michelle gave me the divorce papers yesterday. It was the first time we'd *actually* talked in a while—about right."

His stomach sank. As soon as the detective found out that little piece of information, his brother would be suspect number one. He already would have been number one on the list, but now they would be unlikely to look at anyone else until they could solidly prove that he wasn't responsible—which, in all honesty, Casper wasn't sure they would be able to do.

"Why didn't you tell me?" he asked, already knowing his brother's answer—because Casper had been acting like a jerk and a terrible brother.

All he had done was concentrate on his own grief and anger.

How could he have been so self-righteous?

He continued to beat himself up as he carried the bedding roll downstairs to the laundry and got it started while William kept clearing things up in his bedroom.

Kristin turned off the vacuum and made her way over to him as he poured a lid full of laundry detergent into the washer.

"I'm sorry," she said, touching him gently.

"Are you leaving?" he asked, suddenly afraid by the tone of her voice.

She shook her head. "I will stay to help as long as I can. Roger just texted me, though, and I have to go into his office to discuss the disciplinary plan."

"That's nothing to be sorry for," he said, somewhat relieved that she hadn't said she couldn't deal with all the upheaval and chaos in his family and she had made a terrible mistake in opening up her body and her heart to him last night.

He wouldn't have blamed her, if she had told him to pound sand. His life had hit a new disaster level, one lower than ever before. After the way she had seen him treat William, she probably didn't think he was a man she needed in her life.

Chapter Nineteen

She had made a terrible mistake. They should have waited to share Kristin's bed until she'd had a chance to know Casper better. The man he had appeared to be was a stark contrast to the man who was standing in his brother's house.

He'd made William out to be such a jerk since she had known him, saying that they'd not had a close relationship, and he'd even implied his brother had played a role in his father's death, but looking at his brother now, she couldn't begin to imagine how Casper could have jumped to those kind of conclusions. If anything, his brother was nothing more than a broken man.

She was being unfair, though. So many things happened between brothers, wedges that couldn't be easily explained and that she wouldn't understand. She had to trust her gut in the fact Casper was a great man.

She was so confused. Her heart and her mind

were being pulled in different directions and she hated every second of it.

"Did you come check on your brother after I saw you in the hospital?" she asked, standing with him in the laundry room as he worked to help with his brother's bedding and dirty clothes.

"I didn't." He shoved the soap drawer closed and pushed the buttons to start the machine. "Turns out, I should have."

"Didn't you say your brother and his wife had a nurse coming into their place to help care for your father?"

He nodded.

"Wouldn't they have been helping to keep the place clean and well-kept?"

He sighed. "That was the impression I was under. The last time I was at the house was Thanksgiving. It had been in good shape—*perfect*, actually."

"Caring for a loved one can take a toll on a relationship. Do you think that was what happened between he and Michelle, or do you think it was something else?"

He shrugged. "I can't tell you. All I know is that I didn't really know my brother like I thought I did. I've made a lot of assumptions— wrong assumptions. Assumptions that will haunt me for years to come."

Her heart wanted her to take him in her arms and comfort him, but there was a wave of anger coming off him that seemed to radiate with *don't touch*.

She really had made a mistake. "You did the best you could, with the information you were given."

"Something like that."

She hated the way he sounded. Part of her wanted to shake him out of this funk in hopes she could have back the man she had fallen for.

"I'm going to go."

He nodded, not looking at her as he opened up the dryer and started to fold a load of clothes that were almost hard from sitting in there for so long. "Yeah. I get it."

"If you need anything, call me. A ride, whatever. Let me know when you plan on going back to Big Sky."

"Sure," he said in a clipped tone, but there was a strangled noise in his voice that made her want to turn him around so she could see his face.

If she did that, though, it was possible that she would get sucked back into this in a way she wasn't sure she wanted to be.

They both just needed a moment to think. She had a lot going on in her life and as much as she wanted to help him, after this week, she was already going to be doing a lot of cleanup. To be hit with this level of family drama on top of it all... Well, maybe this relationship wasn't something she wanted. Sure, she wanted to be there for Casper, but it would come at one hell of a cost to herself. It already had.

Turning away, she made her way out of the house and it wasn't until she was outside that she found she could breathe. There was so much going on in there, so many feelings, so many questions, that it was suffocating. After getting into her car, she picked up her phone and texted Roger that she was on her way.

As she drove, she couldn't help but feel like she had let Casper down, but he hadn't argued when she told him she was going to go.

When she arrived at the SAR building, Roger was already there. His truck was parked outside, along with a number of other cars she recognized as belonging to the chief and the rest of the board. This was going to be a long afternoon. Hopefully, though, she could learn more about Michelle's death.

When she made her way inside, Roger was sitting with the board in the meeting room. It was a glass room in the center of the building with drop-down blinds for privacy that no one ever seemed to use. If they did, someone was getting fired. If anything, it was a good sign that they weren't already drawn.

Her stomach ached.

She tapped on the wooden door and Roger waved her inside.

"Hey, guys," she said, sounding less confident than she would have liked, but unable to summon anything more than she was feeling.

The three other members of the board gave her a curt welcome.

She sat down next to Roger, unsure if she wanted to be so close to the man wielding the axe.

Roger gave her a tip of the head, but his face was impassive.

"Any word on the cause of death?" she asked, trying to quell the ache in her gut.

Roger looked at the others sitting at the table, but no one seemed to want to meet his gaze. The head of the board and the woman to his left, Mayor Marcy Davis, looked over at Kristin and smiled. "Actually," she began, "we were hoping to ask you a few questions about her and your actions that led to locating her body."

"Absolutely, I'm happy to answer." She tried to smile, but it didn't take.

Roger started to say something but Marcy cut him off with a sharp look.

"Roger, here," Marcy continued, "said that

you blatantly ignored his orders in going outside the search perimeter after you had conducted your initial search track and had been asked to rest. Is that accurate?"

She squirmed slightly in her seat, but she hoped they didn't notice. "I wouldn't say we *blatantly* did anything. My teammate's dog had gone missing. It would have been unethical and morally questionable to stop searching at that time."

Marcy smiled, but Kristin couldn't make heads or tails if the action was friendly or malicious, and that only amplified her anxiety.

"You didn't listen to my orders. You could have put more people at risk by acting on your own accord." Roger looked furious.

"For that, I do apologize. I can see your concern, sir," Kristin said in earnest. "I wasn't aware that we were going to cause a problem for you. If we'd known, I can promise that we wouldn't have taken a risk. As it was, we are both well-trained in self-rescue and in search techniques and we felt comfortable in continuing our search not only for the missing woman, but also the dog."

"I consider you a friend as well as a colleague," Roger continued, not really seeming to listen to her apology. "As such, I think you just assumed that you could do as you wished without fear of reprisal."

"Sir, I wouldn't wish to compromise our work or our friendship in any way."

"Both of you," Marcy interjected, "let's talk about why we are really here. Roger informed us that he put you on a leave as a result of your actions. That being said and after further review, the board and myself have decided not to enforce the punishment and reinstate you fully."

She smiled widely. "Thank you. I appreciate—"

Marcy put her finger up, silencing her. "That being said, we do not condone your cavalier actions. In this case, we see validity in your argument and in the fact that you and your teammate found the missing woman."

Suddenly, the truth of the situation hit her. *This could have been easily resolved in a phone call. They wanted me face-to-face for another reason.*

"As of late, you have been involved with a number of *interesting* events."

She gripped her hands together tightly in her lap, under the conference table. "Yes, but—"

"We know that you are not the cause of any of these events," Marcy said, cutting her off, "but it is odd that you are at the center of so much."

She looked down at the table.

Roger tapped his pencil against a pad of paper that she hadn't noticed he had been writing on.

"We are concerned for your well-being." Marcy reached over like she wanted to touch her, but then retracted her hand.

She jerked as she looked up at Marcy. "Why? What do you mean?"

Marcy opened up a yellow file resting in front of her. "We received the mechanic's report on the helo after it went down in Big Sky." She flipped to a picture of a mess of black hydraulic lines and turned it so she could see. "If you look here," she said, pointing toward an opening in a black line, "they found clear evidence of not breakage, but what appeared to be an intentional cut mark."

Holy crap.

"What?" Kristin choked on the question.

"There were marks on a couple of the other hydraulic lines as well. As if, whoever was responsible had been making sure that at least one of the lines would fail midflight."

"That doesn't make sense." Kristin shook her head. "No one at that location or in Billings would have wanted to compromise our bird."

"We think that it may have had something to do with you. Maybe Casper?"

The blood drained from her face. Casper. Someone was targeting *Casper.*

Of course, they were. Why didn't I put it to-gether?

"Did you see anything? Anyone who seemed to have a problem with your teammate?" Roger asked, his tone taking on a new softness.

Her first thought went to Greg, but he hadn't really had a problem with Casper—aside from the fact he had taken his bird. That was a pretty big thing, but at the same time Greg had signed up for the training with the knowledge that he may not be the only person operating the helo. It would have been against his own self-interest to make a move like this.

She stared at the picture.

"How long do you think the cuts would have held before breaking?" she asked, though she wasn't sure that they would really have an answer.

"It's tough to say," Marcy said. "According to the mechanic's findings, it would have been dependent on the pressure the aircraft was under and the stress of the flights."

A terror filled her. "Okay, but do you think it happened here in Billings…before we ever went their direction for training? On our last rescue mission, we were only flying for about an hour and then it was about an hour to Big Sky. Neither flight was in harsh weather or with much altitudinal changes."

"It sounds like you are thinking it happened in advance?" Marcy countered.

She shrugged, letting out a long sigh as she tried to order her thoughts. "There is no way I could know anything for sure, but I don't think I have anyone who would really wish me harm. Casper, on the other hand, like you said, he's had a lot going on his life recently. The last mission we went on before travel and training was the one in which we were looking for his father. My hang-up is that Casper wasn't on that flight."

"Who was on the flight with you?" Marcy asked.

The other board members at the table looked anxious. The man to her left was scratching at the back of his neck and the other was chewing at his lip. Apparently, no one at the table was very pleased with the conversation they were having.

"On the flight to locate Hugh Keller we had three on board—myself, a nurse and our pilot, Greg." She winced at the sound of his name. "As some of you may know, I'm aware that Roger does at the very least, Greg and I had been dating until a few months ago. Things were amicable between us and I don't think he would wish me any harm."

"Wow." Marcy sat back in her chair as she

studied her. "You were quick to explain the situation between you and Greg. Is there a reason for that?" Her question came off as more of an accusation than a query.

"I just don't want anything to come out later that would give our organization a black eye."

"And we do appreciate that." Roger nodded.

The other two men at the table mumbled in agreement.

Marcy shuffled the papers in the folder on the table. "So…this Casper. What is the nature of your relationship with him?"

No… Why did she have to ask? Was it even any of their business?

"We are friends," she said, trying not to let the truth flare on her cheeks. She and Casper's relationship didn't need to be on trial here.

"Did you know the deceased?" Marcy asked.

She shook her head.

"What about Michelle's husband, Casper's brother…" She fluttered through the file as if it held the man's name.

"William. Yes, I met him today." Her entire body stiffened at the mention of him, but she didn't really know why.

"How did you meet him?" Roger asked.

Again, she wasn't sure why they would be asking all these questions.

"We went over to check on his welfare. After

I texted you and you told me he had been notified by law enforcement of her death, Casper wanted to see him."

"And you were with Casper this morning?" Marcy asked, like she could see right through her and to the reality that Kristin had spent the last night in his embrace.

Thankfully, Roger didn't wait for her to answer. "In what state did you find him… William, that is?"

"His place was a dumpster fire. We ended up helping him to clean it up a bit."

Roger's jaw dropped. "You did what, now?"

She frowned, wondering why he'd had such a strong reaction to an innocuous thing. "We helped him throw out some trash. You know, picked up his place."

"I heard you the first time." Roger ran his hands over his face in exasperation. "You do realize that he is under investigation for his wife's murder?"

"What?" She was genuinely confused.

"So…in helping to clean up what very well may be a crime scene," Roger stated, "you may have just become an accessory, after the fact."

Chapter Twenty

He was petting Grover and William was in the shower when Casper's phone rang. Kristin was in a panic when he answered. "Someone cut the hydraulic lines. You were right, someone out there wants one or both of us dead," she said, her words becoming almost one as she spoke.

"What is going on? Are you okay?" He tried to remain calm, though his anxiety immediately spiked and Grover hopped down from the couch, going on alert.

"I'm fine, but you have to stop whatever you are doing at William's."

He looked around the living room. "What do you mean?"

"Your brother is being investigated. They think he may have done something to Michelle and…"

"Are you kidding me?" The ache in his gut returned.

"You called it with him." There was the slam

of a car door in the background of the call. "I'm on my way back to you. You need to get out of there."

"I didn't call anything." He sank deeper into his brother's couch, listening for a moment until he could once again make out the sounds of his brother's shower going overhead. "My brother didn't have anything to do with Michelle's death. You saw him. He was destroyed."

"Destroyed or not. In helping him with his place, we have just made ourselves possible accessories after the fact in a homicide."

He shook his head, disbelieving. "No. No way." The knot in his stomach grew as he thought about what she had just told him and the huge mistake they had made in his attempt to help his brother.

"Does your brother have a criminal defense attorney?"

"I have no idea." He stared at the coffee table, still covered in crumbs, as Grover came over to him and nudged his hand.

"Well, if he does, *we* may need their number."

She was overreacting. They hadn't done anything wrong. "We will be fine. My brother is innocent."

"Are you sure? I'm not, Casper." She paused, but he said nothing. "I'll be there in twenty minutes." She ended the call.

He had known it was possible that William would be questioned about Michelle's passing, but he hadn't really thought he would be heavily investigated. From everything he had seen at his brother's house when they'd arrived, he hadn't walked out of that house in weeks. He would be happy to testify to the fact, if push came to shove. He got up and let Grover into the backyard.

William was in his bedroom with the door closed when he charged toward it. He knocked so hard that he heard a picture drop from the wall, its glass breaking as it hit the floor. Normally, he would have felt bad, but right now, he felt no guilt about destroying pieces of his brother's world.

"William? Can I come in? We need to talk." He couldn't wait to really talk to him and get the answers that they all needed...and to learn what had been going on between his brother and Michelle. If he could just give Casper some insight into their relationship, beyond the fact that it had been rocky, maybe he could help William get out of this pinch.

There was no answer.

Maybe William was still in the bathroom, shaving or something.

He knocked again.

No answer.

His heart started to race. His brother had been upset, clearly. He hadn't appeared suicidal when they'd arrived or anytime since—depressed, yes, but he hadn't expressed guilt or a desire to die. William wouldn't have done anything stupid.

He tried to open the door, but found it locked. It didn't budge as he pressed his weight against it, and there was no noise coming from inside.

His heart was thrashing in his chest. His brother was inside. Something was wrong. He pulled out his phone, dialed 911 and then dropped it onto the ground. He backed up as he heard the dispatcher answer, but he didn't care what they had to say—all he needed was for them to send help.

He kicked the door as hard as he could, next to the latch. It took all of his strength, but it busted open, the force breaking the doorjamb and sending cracked wood in a variety of directions as the door flew open.

"William! Where are you?" he called, searching frantically for his brother.

The shower was off in the bathroom, but once again, the door was closed and locked. It didn't take as much force to bust the door open this time. On the floor, in front of the shower, was his brother. He had a towel wrapped around his body and vomit was slipping down his face.

"What did you do, William?" He fell to the floor by his brother, pulling him into his lap and doing a sweep of his mouth to clear it of anything that could possibly choke him. He tried to find a pulse, but failed. His was racing so much, though, that he worried he wouldn't have been able to feel it even if it had been as fast and erratic as his own.

His brother was limp as he moved him to the floor.

"Send medical help!" he screamed, hoping the dispatcher would hear him and know to send an ambulance.

Maybe his brother wasn't as innocent as he had hoped, or as guilty as he had once assumed.

PULLING AROUND THE corner and onto the block, Kristin was met with the distinctive red and blue lights of law enforcement and panic washed through her. The house was surrounded by an ambulance and several police cars as Kristin pulled up to William's place. Grover was peeking through the fence, panting, as he watched all the people come and go from the house.

She hadn't been gone for her meeting that long. What could possibly have happened?

Picking up her phone, she tried to dial Casper, but her call went straight to voice mail.

He wasn't dead. He couldn't be.

No one wanted to hurt the brothers, no matter what her bosses had said, no matter what the evidence said… They were just experiencing a wave of bad luck—that was it, nothing more. Or, at least she would have tried to continue to convince herself, but there was no denying there was something going on—something that could very well cause them all to lose their lives, even her.

Regardless, she couldn't leave Casper. She had to protect him even if it cost her life. She didn't care. He wasn't perfect, he had a lot happening in his world, but that didn't mean he was the cause of it or that she could hold it against him. If anything, he needed her to protect him, to help him get through this gauntlet in his life.

And right now, that meant getting into that house and making sure that he was okay. If he wasn't…well, she would cross that bridge when she got there, but needless to say there would be hell to pay to whomever had done him harm.

She parked her car down the street, her tennis shoes grinding in the dirt on the sidewalk as she ran toward the house. There was an officer standing guard and securing the scene, and he put up his hand in a feeble attempt to stop her.

"Excuse me, ma'am," he called toward her as she approached the house. "You need to stop right there."

She said nothing and sprinted toward the front door of the house.

"Ma'am. Stop. Right. There. Get down!" the officer ordered.

She should have responded, but she couldn't. Her body wouldn't let her stop her advance toward Casper. He needed her. Before she reached the doorknob, the cop grabbed her from behind, throwing his shoulder into her and tackling her to the ground. Grover barked from the backyard, like he was trying to help.

Her face cracked hard against the ground, and grass and dirt filled her mouth as she tried to explain in muffled garbles that she had to get inside. She was sure the officer couldn't understand her, and as he pressed his body weight into the middle of her back, pain shot through her.

"I'm sorry," she said in a breathless wheeze.

The officer eased his pressure on her spine. "What's your name?"

"I'm Kristin Loren. I'm a member of the Yellowstone County SAR team. I was just here with another member of my team and I am concerned for his welfare." She tried to sound as professional as possible.

"As a first responder in this county, what in the hell were you thinking?" The officer stood up and dusted off his knees as she stared up from the ground at him.

"I…" The truth was that she wasn't thinking, she was acting. Acting in a moment of pressure was what she had been trained to do. "I was relying on instincts. I apologize. I just…"

"You lost your damned mind." The cop extended his hand and helped her to standing. "You know, thanks to how you acted, I'm going to need to see some ID." He held out his hand as if he expected her to have her driver's license in her back pocket.

"I don't have it on me," she said, motioning toward her SUV. "It's back there in my purse. If you want to walk with me, I'd be happy to show you."

He sighed. "What exactly were you trying to accomplish by getting into the house?"

"I need to know that Casper and his dog are okay."

"Casper?" the officer said, frowning. "Give me a sec. You stay right here, got it?" he asked, pointing at the spot where she stood.

"I got it. I just need to know he is safe."

He clicked on his handset and started to talk as he walked away. His voice was muffled, but she could tell that he was asking about Casper's status.

There was static from the headset and she could hear something about EMS, but beyond that it was too garbled.

Finally, the officer turned around and walked back to talk to her. "So according to the officers inside the house, Casper is unhurt. He is giving a statement about what transpired here today."

"Which was?" she asked, some of the panic she was feeling starting to twist away.

"We are just bringing William Keller out to transport him to the medical-care facility, but it appears that he was either drugged or tried to commit suicide."

Drugged or suicide?

William hadn't been doing well, but she hadn't gotten anything from him that would have made her worry about him self-harming. If anything, he had seemed to perk up and be grateful that she and Casper had arrived to help him.

The thought made her think of Roger and Marcy... Maybe she hadn't helped in the way she had intended—instead, she may well have helped him destroy evidence and get herself wrapped up in a murder investigation that would end with her going to jail.

She had to be reasonable. Though she hadn't approached the scene with as much grace and aplomb as she would have wished, she needed to pull it together now...especially if she was going to come under some kind of investigation in response to all of this.

"Like I said, Officer, I'm incredibly sorry. I'm just extremely tired." She tried to force a stretch and a yawn, but she was sure that he saw right through it. "I was out all night helping with that lost woman. You know, the one we found dead."

He nodded. "Oh, yeah, I heard about that one. Sounds like she might have gotten clipped."

She motioned toward the house. "This is her estranged husband's place."

The officer opened his mouth in surprise. "Oh, damn. I had no idea. You think that's why he tried to possibly off himself?"

She was glad that they had a professional camaraderie going, but she didn't really want to play this game. Yet, there were limited options if she wanted to get her hands on Casper and see that he was, in fact, okay.

"There have been a lot of odd things happening in connection to this family."

"And you want to go in there?" The officer scowled at her.

"Only to make sure that my flight partner is still alive. I have a feeling that with enough time, he could be the one getting clipped next." She wasn't sure where her admission had come from, but she felt the truth of her words in her bones. It seemed as though someone wanted every member of this family dead, but she couldn't understand why, no matter how hard she tried to piece it all together.

The front door to the house opened and the EMS team brought out William, strapped down, on the gurney. His eyes were closed and she couldn't tell if they been able to bring him back to consciousness, or if was still at risk of death. Depending on what he had taken, or was given to him, there could be any number of effects and only a few outcomes—she hoped this time he would come out of it on the full-recovery side.

Following William, Casper walked out. His face was colorless and his shoulders sagged. He helped the EMS workers move his brother down the steps and watched them as they wheeled him to the ambulance and loaded him up. He looked over at her and then stared back at the ambulance like he wasn't sure if he should come to her, or get in the vehicle with his brother.

She walked toward him, noticing what looked like vomit on the legs of his pants. She could only imagine what he had been forced to deal with while he had waited for everyone to arrive.

"Casper…" She said his name softly and just loud enough to break him from his stupor. "If you want to go with your brother, I can grab Grover and follow you guys there."

"My buddy is going to come get Grover. He'll watch him for a few days while I take care of things." He shook his head. "I need to at least keep him safe."

"You didn't have anything to do with that, did you?" she asked, motioning her chin in the direction of William's house.

"Are you kidding me? Are you really asking me if I tried to kill my brother?"

She hadn't meant it like that—*accusatorial*. "No. Casper. I'm sorry. I didn't."

He turned from her, walking until he disappeared into the belly of the ambulance and out of her life.

Chapter Twenty-One

After she had handed off Grover to Casper's friend, she sat outside the emergency room. Every thirty minutes for the first three hours, she sent a text off to Casper, trying to let him know that she was in her car and waiting for him, and to text back if he needed anything from her. After the sixth text with no response, Kristin couldn't stand it any longer and made her way inside.

As she approached the secretary's desk, it struck her that the last time she had stepped foot in a hospital had been the day she had met Casper—the day his father had died. She silently prayed that history wouldn't, once again, repeat itself.

The college-aged woman behind the desk looked up at her, a tired look on her face, as if she was just a few hours from getting to go home and wishing that she was anywhere but behind the plated glass leading to the triage area. Or maybe she was projecting her own feelings onto the poor woman.

"Hi," she said, "I'm Kristin…" She paused, trying to decide if she should give her real name to the woman, knowing that if she did that, she would likely be turned away without ever getting a chance to see Casper and check on William because of privacy laws. "I'm Kristin Keller," she lied, but somehow saying the name made a warm and cozy feeling spread through her. "I'm here to see my brother-in-law, William Keller. I think he was brought in a few hours ago."

The woman nodded, not seeming to notice Kristin's best attempt at a lie. Instead, she started clicking on her keyboard. She handed back Kristin her ID and relief filled her as she slipped the card back in her wallet. "Yep, we have admitted him. It looks like they are just about to transfer him up to the floors."

"Which floor?" Kristin held her breath. If the woman said ICU, then it meant that William was still struggling for his life, but if it was a step-down or medical/surgical unit, then there was a chance they were just keeping him for observation and IV fluids.

The woman clicked on her keyboard and tapped downward a few more times, and as she did so, each tap was like a slice of a blade on Kristin's soft skin. "It looks like he just made it up to room 331. It's on the third floor—take a left and it will be a way down on your left."

"Thank you," she said, waving as she hurried toward the stairs.

She took the steps two at a time, her legs burning as she ascended the last flight of stairs. She was winded as she hit the door to the third floor and burst out in the ICU.

The place was abuzz with the sound of dry IV pumps and the shrill alarms of cardiac and respiratory monitors. She wondered if anyone ever really got used to the cacophony of sounds and they just became white noise.

She made her way down the hallway until she came to 331. The room was surrounded by glass, but the shades were pulled, obscuring everything inside. She tapped on the door, but before anyone answered, a nurse came down the hallway and cut her off.

"Hi, how can I help you?"

"I'm here to see my brother-in-law, William Keller," she lied again, this time the lie coming out with greater ease.

The nurse frowned as he looked at the door and then back to her. "We only allow one guest in the room at a time, due to safety concerns. Right now, I believe he already has a visitor."

She nodded, but she didn't really care what the hospital's arbitrary policies entailed.

"Can you please tell Casper I'm here?" she said quickly, as if every second she stood in the hallway was a second they grew closer to trouble and further loss.

"Sure," the nurse said, holding up his hand. "Wait here."

The man disappeared into the room. It seemed to take forever, even though she could hear the murmur of men's voices coming from inside. Finally, the nurse stepped out, Casper in tow.

"Thank you," Casper said to the nurse. He waited for the man to walk away before he finally turned to her.

"Do you have your phone with you?" she asked, hoping that his lack of the device was why he had hadn't answered.

He patted his chest pockets and then the back pockets of his jeans, finally pulling out his phone and clicking it on. "Yeah." He clicked the buttons. "Sorry, I didn't look at it," he said flatly.

"I'm sorry about the thing I said at the house earlier," she said, trying to right her major wrong.

He looked away from her and toward the door leading to William. "He hasn't regained consciousness. They Narcaned him and got him breathing. They pumped his stomach when he got here, but they aren't sure what he took. There were so many pills in the bathroom and the house that it could have been any combination of things."

She grimaced, wanting to ask if they thought he would make it, but also not wanting to know the answer if it hurt Casper any more than he was already hurting. "Are you going to stay the night with him?"

He looked down at his watch, seeming to realize most of the day had passed in the chaos. "I don't know yet. I'm hoping that he regains consciousness, and I want to be here for him when he does. I need to talk to him."

She remained silent, though she wanted to ask him so many questions.

"The paramedics said they couldn't be certain from the scene whether or not he had intentionally ingested the pills or if he had accidently overdosed. There were no spilled pills or suicide notes. I found him down in the bathroom after his shower. I didn't see any open bottles or anything."

"Then what made them decide it was an overdose instead of another kind of medical emergency?"

"They weren't one-hundred-percent sure until they gave him Narcan. He came around a little bit and his blood pressure started to climb. I thought he was going to come out of it, but he plateaued at one-ten over seventy-two, and his oxygen saturation leveled around ninety-eight percent, and everything has stayed there since he was brought here. They said Narcan only works on opioids, so it's possible that the overdose was on multiple medications."

"How long do they think it will take him to come around completely?"

"If he didn't poison himself, he may come around in a couple days. However, they are probably going to want to get a psych eval. The doc warned me that most people leave AMA, against medical advice, before they can be treated for mental-health problems. And, I fear that if he leaves, he will be arrested as soon as he steps out the doors."

"Wouldn't they have to charge him with something in order to arrest him?"

"His trying to commit suicide is circumstantial. I don't think they have any physical evidence that he actually tried to kill anyone or had any role in Michelle's or Dad's deaths. However, I think his attempt would be enough to book him on suspicion. It would give them time to dig without fear that he would run or follow through on his suicide attempt."

"If it helps, I talked to one of the officers outside the house. They didn't even know he was in any way involved with Michelle. I don't think he was even on their radar as a suspect."

He tipped his head in acknowledgment, but his face pinched. "He may not have been, but he definitely is now. If I was the detective on this case, I would be on him after this incident."

"I know you said you thought he did have something to do with her death, until you saw his place. Then you did an about-face. What made you change your mind...or did you?"

He leaned his body against the wall and looked down the hallway. The nurses had all retreated to other patients' rooms or the nurses' station, far enough away to be out of earshot. "I can't say he didn't do it with complete certainty, but I can say that I've never seen him so screwed up. I've lived with him off and on throughout the years—college, breakups and our mother's death—and he's never just *given up*."

"Do you think that this odd behavior is indicative of wrongdoing?"

"If you mean that he murdered someone, I don't think so. She had served him with divorce papers around the time our father died. I think it was the combination of factors that did him in."

She sucked in a breath. "She did *what*?"

"Oh, yeah, she served him with papers the day she went missing."

She couldn't take the way his face fell as he

spoke. "Casper, I'm so sorry," she said, moving closer, silently begging for his reassuring touch.

He took the little step toward her. "I'm just glad you're here," he said, pulling her into his arms and against him until she could feel him breathe into her hair. "I'm surprised they let you in."

There was just something about that action that she loved. It was like he was breathing her in and she was a part of him, and in that moment, even though it wasn't the physical entwining of bodies, they were still one—two halves of a greater whole. "I may have fibbed a little and said you and I were married." She looked up at him and smiled.

"Oh," he said, sounding surprised. There was a pause. "What happened with your board meeting?"

She let him hold her as she stared into his eyes. "We discussed the cut hydraulic lines."

He nodded stoically. "Do they know who was responsible?"

She shook her head, but her thoughts went straight to Greg. "My board is worried that there may be someone targeting your family."

"Anything is possible," Casper said, sounding resigned.

There was a shrill beep from William's hospital room. "Do you think it would be better if I stepped back? You know…so I could keep my drama out of your life? You have enough on your plate without my garbage."

He held her tighter. "I need you. I need your insights. You can do what you want, and you can go if you want, but know that there is no question in my mind about you and how important you are to me. You've been there for me through this, a time when I needed so much support. You're the only person standing strong and staying by my side."

He acted like she really had a choice…but didn't he understand that her heart wouldn't have allowed her to make any other decision? She had been inextricably linked to him since the moment she had first seen him in the hospital. Ever since then, the world and their lives had only strengthened the signs that they were meant to be exactly where they were, exactly right now.

"I need you, too," she said, taking his face in her hands and giving him a kiss.

He kissed her like he was a man starving, searching in a desert of abandonment and pain, and finally finding her and the fullness of her promises.

A nurse walked by and cleared his throat, and she pulled out of Casper's embrace, once again remembering where they were and what was going on around them. Now wasn't the time or the place.

"Casper?" she said, her voice slightly raspy.

"Hmm?" He closed his eyes as he tipped his head back, moving his face so it was out of her view and making her wonder what all he was feeling, yet not wanting to cause him pain by poking at a sensitive spot.

Yet, there was no avoiding certain things. "I think we need to get ahead of the investigation."

"Is this because of the meeting with the board? Did they say something I need to know?"

She let the silence speak for itself.

He dropped his chin and she watched as the storm came back into his eyes. "What is it that you think we should do?"

She shook her head. "I don't really know, but I'm thinking that the best thing we can do is try and find out what happened to Michelle. Depending on how that goes, we can pivot from there. But, if there's any truth to what people are saying, and she was murdered and William is the primary suspect, then we need to either clear his name or clear our own."

He sucked in a long breath, holding it in as he paused to think. "What if we dug into my dad's death?"

"When it comes to his passing, the only person who could really answer any questions… well, he is unconscious." She took his hand.

He nodded, but there was pain on his face like she had lanced him with her words.

"I'm sorry, Casper... I didn't mean to be callous—"

"That's not it. You're right. I know you're right. I just hate it—*all* of it." He gripped her. "I wish you could have met my family a few years ago, before my mother passed and everything went to hell."

"When a family goes through a shake-up, it rocks everyone to their foundation. Everyone has to rebuild, we all hope for something strong and better, but the truth is that many families collapse." She took his other hand and looked him in the eyes. "It is in those moments you have to dig deep. You have to find your own way, and do the best you can for yourself and for those who are still part of your life."

"You...are the one still in my life." He stared into her eyes. "I want to do the best we can, together. We will figure this all out."

She smiled, but her heart was breaking. "First, focus on *you*. You need to come back stronger and better for *you*. Then, we can be the strongest *we* that we can be." Tears started to form in her eyes, but she feared letting them fall in front of him. He needed a place of respite, not a continuing disaster.

Chapter Twenty-Two

Casper wasn't sure how he had found himself standing inside the local sheriff's department. Yet, as they walked to Detective's Terrell's office, there was no turning back now. Kristin had wanted this, and he had to agree that she was being smart—they needed to get in front of the investigation and keep any fallout from coming back on them.

Detective Terrell motioned for them to take a seat. "So you are Michelle Keller's brother-in-law? And you, Kristin, had a hand in finding his father while working with our SAR team?" He looked from Casper to Kristin.

She nodded.

"Does your team's law-enforcement coordinator know that you have decided to show up in my office?" he asked, frowning.

"She's not the person who needs to worry about being in the wrong here, or at least I'm here to tell you that she is free of any guilt. I'm here to clear our names and see if there is anything we can do to actively help in your investigation of Michelle's death." He wanted to say "investigation into his father's death" as well, but he needed to know where this man stood before he opened himself up.

"Why do you think you'd need to clear your names?" The detective worked on his computer, probably pulling up the report from Michelle's disappearance.

By now there had to be several reports filed, and maybe they would even have the date and time of the autopsy.

"We—*I*—made a mistake." Casper rubbed the back of his neck.

"Oh?" Detective Terrell looked up at him.

He didn't know how much detail the man needed and he didn't want to throw his brother under the bus if they weren't already looking in his direction. Maybe they had made a huge mistake in coming here.

"What he is trying to say is that he is interested in learning more about the findings as to the cause of Michelle's death. Was it homicide or accidental?" Kristin leaned forward like she was putting her body between Casper and the firing squad.

There were some bullets that she didn't need to take.

"Is there some reason you believe it would have been a suicide?"

Casper looked at the man's badge. "Detective, I know that you are doing your job... I get it. I would, however, appreciate if you would let me know what you have, so I know where to start."

Terrell smiled, the action not threatening but not entirely friendly. "As I'm sure you know, her death is under active investigation."

"When we found her," Casper began, more anxious now that when they had arrived at the sheriff's office, "she had blood around her mouth. Do you know what caused it?"

"From our initial findings, she had a series of broken ribs. One of which punctured her lung."

"Was that the cause of death?" Kristin asked.

Terrell shrugged. "I can't give you any answers to that right now, until we get through her autopsy."

"Is it scheduled?" Casper asked.

"Tomorrow," Terrell said.

"She smelled of chemicals," Casper added. "Do you know what could have caused it?"

Terrell shook his head. "Again, I won't know until tomorrow, but I included the scent in my report." Terrell's phone pinged and he looked at it and frowned, making Casper wonder if they were keeping him from doing other, more important things.

"We can just get out of your hair," Casper said, moving toward the door of the man's office. The place wasn't very big, and when he turned, the chair behind him slammed against the wall and made the pictures beside the man's desk rattle against the wall.

Terrell stood up and touched his framed picture of George Washington, then straightened it slightly, like it was a part of him that Casper had unwittingly disturbed.

He definitely wasn't ingratiating himself with the guy. "Sorry. I just bumped the—"

Terrell stopped him with a raise of his hand. "No matter. And, no, you don't need to go anywhere, so please sit back down. I'm here to help your sister-in-law by getting answers about her death. If you think you can help me, and bring peace to those who loved her, then I would be glad to hear what you have to say."

Kristin grimaced as Casper folded back down into the hot seat.

"Let me start by saying I think my brother, Michelle's husband, is innocent of any crime. He is in a dark mental place, but I think it is because of her and not because of what happened to her."

"What makes you say that about your brother?" Terrell tented his fingers in front of him on the desk, giving them his full attention.

"I'm not here to get my brother in trouble, but it's important that we be as transparent as possible." As quickly as he could, he explained the divorce papers and how they had cleaned his brother's house.

Terrell sat back slightly, taking in all the information. "Did you see anything while either of you were cleaning up that would lead you to believe that William wished Michelle harm?"

They both shook their heads.

"It was mostly food garbage, but I helped him throw a few loads of laundry into the machine… and some sheets."

Terrell's eyebrows rose, but then his normal, unflappable expression returned. "Did you see anything that looked like blood or any other form of bodily fluids on the sheets or mattress?"

Casper shook his head. "Like I said, I didn't see anything. My brother's place was just a disaster. It looked like he had been living on his own for at least a month."

"Wait—" Terrell turned back to his computer and clicked on a few buttons "—didn't I see somewhere that your father had been staying with your brother and his wife until he slipped from the home? He, your father, died of a heart attack? Yes?"

He wasn't ready to open up a whole can of worms, but there was no going back now. "I hate to say it, but I'm worried that my father may have been out of the house for a longer time than my brother reported. If you look at the report about my father's disappearance and rescue by SAR, he was quite a distance from the home and he was wearing ripped and tattered clothing."

"What is it that you are saying, Mr. Keller?" The man stared at him like he was reading every twitch on his face and trying to see if he was telling the truth or something else.

"I'm saying that my brother was clearly suffering from some mental-health issues. I think that it is very possible that my father walked away from the house. I don't think my brother would intentionally have neglected my father, but it appears that Michelle had left the home some time before my father went missing."

Kristin reached over and put her hand on his back and he leaned into her reassuring touch. It was amazing how a simple touch could calm his nerves.

They were doing the right thing. His brother could get the help he needed and they could all get the answers to hopefully clear his name.

Terrell opened up another file on his computer. "I'm sure I can get in touch with her lawyer and see when she had first started talking to them about filing for divorce. They may not tell us anything, but as this is now a death investigation, they may be willing to help in at least providing us with dates. We can go from there, and get your brother cleared as quickly as possible."

Casper nodded in agreement. "I think that would be great."

Kristin's face tightened, like she wanted to say something, but was holding back.

"What are you thinking, Ms. Loren?" Terrell asked, obviously noticing the same thing Casper did.

She pulled her hands into a tight ball in her lap. "Are there any other leads as to who may have played a role in Michelle's death?"

Terrell shook his head. "Not at this time, but we have been in contact with Michelle's boyfriend."

Casper tried not to give away his shock. *She had a boyfriend?*

That changed a few things.

"What was her boyfriend's name? How long had they been together?" Casper asked, questions flooding through him. "It's important that we know if this guy is behind things… If he is coming after us."

Terrell shook his head. "At this time, I'm not at liberty to share that kind of information."

"So this is becoming a criminal investigation?" she asked.

Terrell set his jaw. "I think it would be best if you guys laid low for a bit, until things calm down. We don't know for sure that these events are related."

"They are." Casper could feel it in his bones. "If you care at all about our safety, you need to bring him in."

Terrell tapped his finger on his desk in annoyance. "Look, I want you both to know that I appreciate you coming forward with all of this information."

"Are we allowed to go back into my brother's house?" Casper countered.

"I recommend you don't do anything rash, but yes. As of right now, until we get the autopsy reports and do some legwork, we aren't pursuing any criminal charges. You are free to do as you please, as it isn't officially a crime scene."

Chapter Twenty-Three

Kristin couldn't believe how much better she felt after having left the detective's office, but she wasn't sure she could say the same of Casper. He had a torn expression, one that hadn't changed since they'd left over an hour ago. She had asked him several times if he wanted to talk, but he'd simply shook his head. At dinner, she was hoping he'd open up a bit more, but he'd still refused to talk about things with his brother.

After quickly stopping by his house to let Grover out and checking on his brother, who was still unconscious, he finally spoke up. "Would you mind dropping me off at my brother's place?"

She hit the brakes instinctively. "Are you kidding me?"

He looked at her. "I need to make sure everything is taken care of there. Now that we know we aren't under investigation, I don't see the harm."

"You don't see the harm?" she repeated disbelievingly. The relief she had been experiencing evaporated. "Just because we aren't under investigation *yet* doesn't mean that we won't be. Do I need to remind you that we were only ever planning to get out in front of the thing in hopes to remediate any future issues?"

"I agree, but since we left I've been thinking about our helo. *If* it's related to all of these things that are happening—which, truthfully, I don't know—if it *is*, William wouldn't and couldn't have cut those lines. He doesn't have the knowledge or a reason to want to kill us. He doesn't know you or Greg, and I don't get the impression that he would want me dead."

"Who, other than you, would have the knowledge to down our helo?" As soon as she asked the question, she already knew the answer. "Greg wouldn't want me dead, either," she answered, before he even had time to ask the question she could feel coming.

"Are you sure?" He eyed her.

She didn't want to defend Greg, and she didn't think he was a great man, but the thought of him trying to kill her seemed completely crazy. "Just because two people had a relationship and it ended, it doesn't mean that they hate each other or wish each other harm."

"He was angry, though. You can't deny it."

She thought about bringing up the fact that his brother had a better motive for wanting everyone around him dead—if he was the only person left standing in the family, any and all of their father's death benefits or other inheritance would likely automatically revert to him. If he knew Casper was on the helo, or going to be on a helo, it was easy enough—with a little bit of internet searching—to figure out exactly how to go about sabotaging them. Yet, bringing up his brother right now didn't seem like the right move—not only was it juvenile, but it would also only push them apart.

"I won't deny that there is animosity between us," she admitted. "However, before we start trying to fill in the blanks on what has happened over the last few weeks, let's get solid evidence to support any assumptions."

"Now you understand another reason why I want to go to my brother's house," he said, smiling roguishly. "Last time, I just wanted to help him, but now I want to help all of us. Maybe I can find something he or Michelle left behind… or something that will point us and law enforcement in the right direction."

She didn't have any other ideas, at least any that wouldn't require a search warrant, so she nodded. "If I go along with this, we don't move or change anything. In fact, we should take pictures when we go into the house in case things go sideways."

"Fair," he countered. "I was actually thinking the same thing. I agree that I don't want to make things worse for us. Which brings me to my next point…"

She glanced over at him as she started to drive toward his brother's house. "Which is?"

"In order to protect you from falling under any further scrutiny, especially when it comes to things with Roger and your law enforcement coordinators, maybe it would be best if you didn't go in with me."

She shook her head vehemently. "No."

He paused, waiting for her to elaborate, but she didn't feel like it was necessary to validate her refusal.

"That's it?"

"Yep. You're not going in alone." She shrugged. "If you do that, it's very possible that you could get accused of tampering with evidence in the event we do find something. At least if I'm there, you have some kind of witness."

He sighed, probably because he knew she was right.

The door was unlocked when they got back to William's place. Even if for nothing else, she was glad they could lock things up for him.

It felt strange going in the empty, deathly quiet house. Even though it was cleaned up, it still had an air of unwelcomeness.

"Where should we start?" she asked, hoping they would sift through for clues as quickly as possible.

"I'm thinking I'll go into his bedroom and poke around in his closet to see if he has a lockbox or anything. Why don't you start in his office? I'll meet you in there," he said, pointing down the first-floor hall to where a spare bedroom and the office sat.

"On it." She started to walk away, but he stopped her, spun her around and planted a kiss on her lips.

"Thank you," he said, a softness in his eyes that she had only seen once before—when they were making love.

"You're welcome." There wasn't anything she could think of that she wouldn't do for him. She hated to name what emotion was the motive for her feeling this way.

He let her go, but gave her one more peck as she turned. With that simple action, she felt lighter and less torn about what they were doing. Casper was right—they needed to find the answers.

She hadn't been in the office when they'd been here before and she opened the door to an aroma of rancid food. Holding her breath, she walked to the window and opened it, then did the same in the spare bedroom to help create a cross draft. Making her way back, she started by looking on the chair by his desk. It had a stack of unopened mail, including magazines, bills and political ads. She fanned through the mail, but nothing jumped out at her as important other than the fact that he was probably behind on his mortgage.

Moving to his desk, there was a medley of Chinese food containers and discarded sushi trays. She picked up the trash can and moved to start cleaning up, but as she picked up the first container, she looked in the bin. Inside, on top of used tissues and covered in what looked like coffee grinds, she could make out the top of legal paperwork.

Fishing it out and wiping away some of the coffee grounds that were stuck to the paper, she found that it was a certified copy of Michelle's petition for divorce. Montana was a no-fault state, but it still cited irreconcilable differences.

She flipped through it. There was a list of assets, and as she started to scan it, she immediately started to notice a trend. Before continuing, she put down the bin and made her way out of the office. "Casper!"

She heard the sound of footsteps as he moved

overhead in the main bedroom. "Yeah?" he responded, his sound muffled.

She made her way to the living room so he could hear her better. "I found the divorce filings."

His footsteps sounded loudly as he left the bedroom and made his way down the stairs. "Nice find," he said, making his way to her in the living room.

She handed it over to him, pointing at the assets, where it showed a combined debt of nearly five hundred thousand dollars. "It looks like your brother and his wife were in severe financial distress."

"And right there, we have a motive for my father's murder."

"What? How is that?"

He sighed. "My father had a trust. He had set aside a great deal of cash while he'd been alive and invested it wisely. My brother was the administrator on the trust."

"Is that why he chose to keep your father in his home and under his care…so they didn't have to spend your father's assets on a care facility?"

"Trusts keep a family from losing a loved one's assets or home because of long-term care, but only after five years. It had only been three years since my father had begun the trust. As such, his home and his investments would have had to have been used for nursing care, or they would have been beholden to the government for the cost of his nursing."

"So, yes?"

"Exactly. I told my brother it was better to have my father in a trusted and well-rated care facility, where he could get everything he needed. Sure, he hadn't wanted the money to go to his care and had wished for it to go to those listed in his will and trust, but I didn't want my father to get put in a place where he would be forgotten."

Kristin's chest tightened. "And I'm sure you trusted your brother and his wife to treat your father with the love and care he deserved."

"You know I did," he said, his voice heavy with emotion. "I checked on them all at Thanksgiving and everything was looking good. My father had lost weight and was declining cognitively, but I thought that all had to do with his aging process."

Kristin noticed that the divorce paperwork was shaking in his hands. "It may have been. You don't know. Again, we have to prove anything we are thinking before we erroneously make conclusions."

He gripped the paperwork tightly and slapped it down on the living room table.

"We need to find your father's financials—the ones your brother controlled. If he was spending anything he shouldn't have been spending… then perhaps you are right. We'd still need more proof that he was mistreating your dad or being negligent in his care."

"It may have nothing to do with that, too. We just need to keep digging." Casper stuffed the divorce filing into his back pocket.

"Did you find a safe or anything upstairs?"

He shook his head. "I'm thinking that whatever paperwork my brother has about my father or anything else has to be in his office." He pointed down the hallway.

She made her way back to the office. If nothing else, they were on the right track. Casper followed her inside and started on the bottom left drawer of the desk. The thing was stuffed with files and he started by pulling out the first and sifting through before moving to the next. Going over the stacks of papers on the desk, she set aside anything that could be potentially interesting on further inspection and anything inconsequential on the chair.

When the stack on the chair started to shift and she feared it tipping, she lifted the pile and dropped it to the floor. It wasn't her intention to disrupt William's life any more than it already was, but there was really no system to his paperwork that she could discern—at least not in the last six months.

She glanced over at Casper, who was about halfway through the drawer. He looked so incredibly focused and drool-worthy. She really was an incredibly lucky woman to have found him.

As he moved, she wanted to take him in her arms, kiss him and tell him they would come through this, and that his brother wasn't the monster that all the signs seemed to be making him out to be.

"Did William ever say anything about his and Michelle's relationship to you?"

"He told me he was in love." Casper set down the file in his hand and moved to the next. "Legitimately, he seemed happy."

"What about Michelle?"

He furrowed his brow as if he was struggling to remember. "She was…not super talkative with me. She was working a lot and not around."

"What did you say she did for work?"

He sat down on the floor as he sifted through another stack of papers. "She was an insurance salesperson."

"Okay…" She tried to pull her thoughts together. "Would an insurance person be working on a holiday?"

He shrugged, not seeming to give it a great deal of thought. "William said she had a party to go to. You know…normal stuff."

"But he didn't go with her?"

"No. I was staying here. He said he wanted to hang out with Dad and me."

She leaned against the desk. "Michelle didn't tell him to go with her since you were here to care for your father? Doesn't that strike you as odd?"

He stopped what he was doing. "I see where you are going with this. It is possible that she was already dating this other dude, her current—or the guy who *was* her current—boyfriend. Maybe that is why she didn't care about William going."

She nodded. "That's kind of what I'm leaning toward. I have to tell you, when my mom and dad had anyone else to watch me—especially when there was a holiday party involved—they took the opportunity."

"At the time, though, I thought William wanted to hang out with his younger brother. I don't spend a lot of time with them. You know?"

She gave a stiff nod. "You guys definitely have a complicated relationship."

"It has been, but when push comes to shove, we've always been there for one another."

"Is that why you changed your opinion of him when we got here?"

He nodded. "That's a huge part of it. Like I said, what you saw isn't the man I know." He sighed. "And I'd still like to think that my brother isn't the kind of guy who would hurt his wife. I know this is terrible, but I'm hoping that she fell and her death was just an unfortunate accident at a crappy time."

"I've heard of stranger things happening," she said, trying to give his hopes a boost.

He pulled out the entire desk drawer and put it on the floor between his legs. As he moved, something beige caught her eye. It looked like a large envelope and she leaned down to get a better look. "Casper," she said, pointing. "What's that?"

Looking up, he spotted the envelope. Its edges were taped to the wooden paneling under the desk and, unless someone had done exactly what Casper had, it would have gone completely unnoticed and undetected.

He pulled it out and ripped off the tape. After unfolding the clasp on the manila envelope, he opened it and pulled out a stack of paperwork. "Oh, holy…crap." He looked up at her with wide eyes. "You need to call Detective Terrell—he needs to know my brother isn't our killer."

Chapter Twenty-Four

The two younger deputies had arrived first and Kristin had led them inside and into the office where they had found the paperwork. They had taken a series of pictures and had left them to do their work, and were now on the front porch, waiting. Detective Terrell had been running a few minutes late, but had been beyond grateful when they had reached out. As they stood to wait for him, Casper couldn't help the nerves that were rising within him.

He needed to make sure that William's name was cleared. Better, before he was even awake. It would be one hell of a gift if they could go to him, before he was transferred to the mental-health unit, and tell him that he was cleared of any wrongdoing. Maybe it would help with his recovery.

A part of Casper wondered if that would actually be true. No matter what had happened to Michelle, William would undoubtedly feel as though he played a role.

Perhaps his proving that William wasn't behind her death was more for himself than his brother. Casper needed to know his brother was innocent and still the person whom he had played baseball with in the backyard, the kid whose laugh would wake Mom and Dad in the middle of the night when they were supposed to be sleeping and were instead up playing video games. He couldn't be the man who could willfully end a life.

Detective Terrell pulled up in his black pickup and turned off the engine. After what seemed like an eternity, he stepped out and walked to them on the front step. "Hey, guys, thanks for calling. I'm sorry about my late arrival. I had to take report and it took a little longer than expected."

Casper shrugged off the apology. "No matter. We are just glad you are here now." He reached into his back pocket and pulled out the folded and dirty divorce paperwork, and Kristin handed him the envelope she was holding against her chest.

The detective took the paperwork and flipped through the divorce order first. "That seems pretty normal."

"Yeah," Casper said, "except the part about

the debt. My brother was frugal. I have a hard time imagining how they were that far in credit-card and loan debt. I mean, look…" He pointed at the page where the debts were listed. "The amount owed on the house was only a hundred and four thousand. Everything else is credit cards and personal loans."

"Many people are in debt in this day and age," the detective said. "Don't get me wrong, that is hefty debt, but that doesn't indicate any sort of wrongdoing or illegal activity."

"No," Kristin said, "but it would give some-one motive to kill. At least for the right amount of money…" She pointed at the envelope be-neath the divorce paperwork.

The detective looked around and pointed in-side. "Why don't we make our way into the house. It looks like we are starting to draw a little extra notice." He motioned in the direc-tion of a man and woman across the street who were peering out their window.

Casper followed behind Kristin and the detec-tive. "I'm not sure if it's enough to arrest any-one, but…it's a place to start your investigation."

The detective closed the front door behind them. They heard the sound of the two other officers coming from the office. "Like I said, we haven't made this a criminal investigation until we get the official results back from the medical examiner. I am going to need to step in on the autopsy in another hour."

"You have to have some kind of idea as to what happened to Michelle." Kristin sounded annoyed, but he could tell it was just that she was concerned.

The detective stared at her for a long moment. "Why did you guys come back to the house?"

"You said we were good." Casper rubbed the back of his neck nervously. "Plus, we wanted to make sure the place was locked up. As I'm sure you know, there is more robbery in this area than anyone wants to admit. If people saw William being wheeled out, they would know the place was empty."

"You made it clear that we weren't under investigation. As such, we wanted to help his brother," Kristin argued.

Casper reached over and put his hand on her arm, trying to help keep her calm. "We aren't trying to make waves, Detective. We saw an opportunity not only to help my brother, but your team as well. As it turned out, it was a positive." He motioned toward the envelope. "Take a look."

The detective opened the envelope and pulled out the insurance policy. He scanned it, flipping through the pages.

"If you look, there are three separate policies there," Casper said, waiting for the detective to read.

"Hmm," the detective began, "it states here that there is one for Hugh Keller, Casper Keller and William Keller. That isn't odd."

"No, it's not." Casper sighed. "However, I didn't even know there was a life-insurance policy out in my name, except that which I pay for through the military."

"Again, and I mean this as nicely as possible, there is nothing illegal here." The detective sent him a pitying look.

"Look at who the beneficiary is on the policies," Kristin said, shifting her weight in anticipation.

The detective flipped farther into the first policy. "Michelle Keller." He read the name like it was nothing. "Again, no evidence of a crime. You guys told me that you found something I had to see. This is it?" He lifted the papers accusatorially.

"Did you see the second beneficiary?" Kristin reached up like she wanted to take the papers from the detective's hand, but she stopped herself and let her arm fall back to her side.

The detective went back to the paper. "Greg Holmes."

Kristin made a slight choking sound as the man spoke her ex's name. "That's the pilot of the helo…our helo that went down in Big Sky. A helo that had the hydraulic lines scored so they would break…"

"Oh," the detective said, sucking in a breath. "Are you aware—" he looked up at them "—that this is Michelle's boyfriend?"

Casper couldn't help the smile that broke out on his face. "I wasn't, but when I saw his name…we had a feeling."

"Explain," the detective said, looking back down at the papers. "Why would you have a feeling?"

"Well, respectfully, I'm no detective here," Casper began, "but it finally all clicked into place. All the crap we have been dealing with, all the things that have been happening to my family. At least now, I think I know why."

The detective peered up at him. "Which is?"

Casper tried to control the flux of emotions that had been roiling within him ever since they had found the paperwork. "This is just a guess, but I bet that Greg and Michelle had been seeing each other for at least the last few months. During this time, they accrued a great deal of debt." He motioned toward the divorce paperwork.

"We haven't found anything in this house that would point toward the debt, or what they spent the money on, but we did find William's personal credit-card statements. He hadn't spent any more than he could pay off with his salary each month," Kristin added.

The detective started to nod. "Okay, I'm tracking what you guys are surmising, but… If Michelle was the primary beneficiary on the life insurance policies…"

"I can't prove it, but I think Greg was going for the money the entire time," Kristin said.

"And you dated this man?" the detective countered.

"It wasn't a great relationship."

"When did you break up?"

She shrugged. "About three months ago. It really wasn't a breakup, though, it was more of going our separate ways. We just kind of stopped talking about anything that wasn't focused on work."

"Did he ever give you any indication he wanted you dead, or do you think he was just gunning for Casper?"

Kristin shrugged, but there were tears forming in her eyes. "I wasn't a great girlfriend… I mean it was just a relationship of convenience. There were no hurt feelings, but—"

"He was verbally abusive toward her," Casper said, interjecting. "I don't mean to talk over you, but he treated you like garbage back there at the camp." He looked at the detective. "He isn't a good man. I'm telling you, everything in my entire being is telling me he is the one behind all these deaths."

"Even your father's?"

"I think that my brother has been in such a low place that he may not have noticed if Michelle came and took my father from the home…or if anyone else did. I know he, my father, was supposed to have a nurse who came and went from my brother's. From the way we found the place, they weren't helping with any sort of upkeep."

The detective tapped the paperwork on his fingers. "So you saying you think Greg came in and took your father out of the home?"

Casper shrugged. "I have no idea how my father got to the area in which he was found. I don't. I also can't believe that he got there himself. Even lost, due to his Alzheimer's…"

"Stop," the detective ordered, putting his hand up. "Your brother was the one to report your father missing…according to the 911 dispatcher."

Casper's stomach sank. Maybe their ideas were wrong. If they were, Greg would get the money from the life insurance policies and there was nothing he could do to stop him from benefiting from his father's death.

"Can we listen to the call?" Kristin asked.

"That's always my first action item," Detective Terrell said, pulling out his phone. "I didn't pull anything outside of what we already knew from the call, but maybe you can hear something I missed."

She shrugged. "It's worth a shot."

The detective clicked on his screen and an audio recording started to play. He skipped past the dispatcher and went straight to the man speaking.

"My father, Hugh Keller, escaped from my home this morning," a man said.

"Escaped?" the dispatcher countered.

"He has dementia and somehow made it outside. I tried to look for him, but haven't found him. I'm worried for his safety."

"Dude," Casper said, sucking in a breath.

"What?" the detective asked, stopping the recording.

"That's not my brother's voice." Casper pointed at the phone like it was some kind of fake.

"No, it's not." The color had drained from Kristin's face. "It's not William's... That voice—that's Greg."

The detective opened his mouth and closed it as the news sank in. "Are you one-hundred-percent sure that is Greg Holmes?"

"He sounds like he was just waking up, but

yes," Kristin said, rubbing the front of her throat. "That was him."

The detective slipped the phone back into his pocket. "You guys...you need to get somewhere this man wouldn't know about—get a hotel room. In the meantime, I'm going to run down this lead." He began to walk away, but turned back. "If you need anything, call me directly. Until I see you again, stay safe."

Chapter Twenty-Five

Kristin stared out of the hotel's window and into the distance, where the rimrocks stood like dark reminders that they were hiding out. Grover was sleeping on the room's couch, his snores filling the air. Her entire body hurt, but she wasn't sure why, entirely. It could have been because of the crash, but it struck her as odd that it was just now noticeable. It also could have been from the hike, but they hadn't covered that many miles while looking for Michelle's body.

Michelle's body... Greg's message... She felt as though she was living someone else's life—this couldn't have possibly been her own. Everything had been so normal, even her relationship with Greg—as short-lived and apparently nonmonogamous as it had been.

Based on the way he had treated her, she should have known that she had not been the only woman in his life. He had never spoken to her about the future. He hadn't even wanted to define their relationship or make definite plans. Everything had always been tentative... and now, it all made sense. She had been nothing but a booty call.

It shouldn't have hurt her; a part of her had known from the very beginning with Greg that they weren't anything but bedroom buddies. Yet, he could have just been honest.

She chuffed. He'd also gone on to possibly kill people for money, so maybe the fact he had just used her was better than the alternative.

"Are you okay?" Casper, who was lying on the bed, asked as he looked up from his phone.

She nodded, but the anger and hate roiled within her. "I—I just feel like an idiot."

"Welcome to the club," Casper said, patting the bed next to him. "I had been working under the falsehood that everything was under control in this city. Little did I know how out of control things had become. If I had just been more involved..."

"And if I had just been more observant..." She walked over to the bed and sat down on the edge, touching his stomach over the soft cotton of his shirt. "I owe you an apology—if I had just been more..." She struggled to find the right word. There were a thousand things she should have been better at in the past, but she had never thought that one of them would have been her poor ability to identify a potential killer.

"You are not to blame. From day one, this has been my circus. Your clown and my clown just decided to join forces."

She giggled, the sound unchecked. "He was definitely a clown. Rather, he *is*." She looked over at Casper and some of the pain she had been feeling dissipated. "Have your people said they have seen him?"

"I have been talking with Cindy." He lifted his phone for her to see. "She said that they tried to take him into custody, but by the time they arrived at the camp, he must have caught wind that they were on their way and disappeared."

She dropped her head into her hands. "You have to be kidding me. How would he know that they were coming for him?"

He shrugged. "It's not that big of a camp, privacy is lacking—need I cite your conversation with Greg? All it takes is one person running their mouth and he could have heard everything. Or maybe he had a feeling. Who knows?"

She lied down on the bed and moved into his nook, putting her head on his chest and looping her arm over him. "You don't really think he would be coming for you, do you?"

"I don't think he would be coming for either of us. At this point, if it is proven he had anything to do with Michelle's death or my father's, he won't be getting any of the insurance money."

"When were the policies purchased?" she asked, stroking the smooth cotton that was stretched tight over the muscles of his chest.

"They were all less than a month old. It looks like Greg had purchased them from Michelle's company—they must have had this all planned out well in advance. From everything I've managed to pull together, they had to have been having an affair for at least the last year. Really, it was pretty clever, but I'm sure he didn't think Michelle would hide those policies in her house."

Casper's phone buzzed and she moved aside so he could sit up and answer the call. "Hello?"

There was the sound of a woman's voice coming from the other end of the line and Kristin could make out about every other word, enough to piece together that William had awakened.

"Is he up to seeing a visitor?"

There was more talking, but Casper smiled excitedly. Not waiting, Kristin moved to the side of the bed, then put on her shoes.

Casper hung up, jumped out of the bed and threw on his shoes. "You ready?"

She was glad he was finally starting to smile again. She couldn't handle any more hurting.

They needed things to start going right—especially now that they had the answers they needed.

As they walked out the door, he slapped her playfully on the butt. "You do know that I'm going to need to see you naked again…as soon as possible?" he said, half whispering.

"Oh, do you think that I should let you?" She giggled.

He smirked and the simple action made her knees threaten to give way.

"If it wasn't for my brother, you know we wouldn't be leaving this hotel room right now." He reached forward and gave her ass a squeeze as they made their way down the hall.

"If you're lucky, maybe later I'll let you show me what you are thinking about doing to me. You better be on your best behavior—until then, I'm watching," she teased, swaying her hips as they made their way out to her car.

She loved the way he was looking at her, like she was something he wanted to lick off his lips. Though she didn't know what the future would bring for them, at least she had the guarantee that there would be more.

WHEN THEY ARRIVED at the hospital, they had to park in the underground garage. The lot was about half-full, and there was a couple making their way into the elevator bay. Stepping out of the Durango, her footfalls echoed on the concrete. Though she couldn't quite put her finger on the cause, a sense of dread filled her.

She'd never loved going into hospitals as a guest, but there was something more in the air beyond her normal apprehension. Maybe it was that Greg was somewhere out there, unchecked and dangerous.

As she reached for Casper's hand, there was a strange but unmistakable sound of a gun's slide as someone racked a round into the chamber. The world around her slowed down.

She had to be wrong.

That couldn't have been a gun.

The garage was empty as the elevator closed ahead of them and the couple disappeared. Maybe it had simply been the slide of the metal doors shutting.

Then the heat hit, and the boom. That bang echoed against the concrete until it was a deafening maw of inescapable terror.

Casper pushed her down to the ground and dropped beside her. She belly-crawled behind the nearest car until she was behind a tire. Casper moved beside her, by the opposite tire.

"Are you okay?" he asked, fear in his voice.

She nodded, putting her hands to her belly. Her shirt was hot and *sticky*.

Lifting her hand, she stared at the dark red blood on her fingers.

I've. Been. Hit.

Her hands started to shake as the pain cascaded through her. Someone had shot her, but why? She hadn't done anything wrong. She didn't even have a gun on her.

She had to fight back.

"I'm fine," she whispered to Casper, lying, as she put her hands down so he couldn't see the blood. As she spoke, a fresh wave of pain coursed through her. He couldn't know she was hurt—it would only make her a burden.

"Do you have a gun on you?" she asked, hoping he was carrying.

He shook his head.

It was too late now, but in the future she would never be without a gun again. Why hadn't she thought to bring one with her, knowing Greg was out there?

She closed her eyes, wishing she could go back and do so many things over again. The pain pulled her down into the darkness of her mind.

Though she had thought about how she would die, bleeding out in a concrete garage beneath a hospital had never hit the list of imagined possibilities.

"If you come out, Casper. I will let her live,"

a man yelled, his voice echoing like the shot, and though it wasn't as loud, it was almost as terrifying.

Casper moved like he was going to step out into the open.

"No!" she ordered. "You're going to be a target for this guy to kill you. I won't allow that." She scanned the ground around them, looking for anything that could be used as a weapon. Her cell phone and her keys were still in her hand. "Here—" she slid her phone on the ground to Casper "—call 911."

He grabbed the phone and dialed the number and hit send before dropping the phone on the ground. The dispatcher's voice filled the air and she found a tiny amount of comfort in the knowledge the police would be on their way.

"Casper is down!" she yelled into the garage, hoping the man would believe her.

There was the sound of laughter. "You know, your taste in men is ridiculous. First, you banged me… Which let's both just say was *subpar*," Greg said, mirth in his chortle. "Then you decide to screw this piece of garbage."

Casper leaned over toward her. "We need to move. He is using our sound to track us. If he finds us, we are dead. I'll take point, and you follow me."

She nodded, ignoring the fire radiating from

the round in her abdomen. Trying to hide her wound from Casper, she gingerly stood up. On the concrete pillar next to her was a large, red fire extinguisher. She pried it loose, the metal making a clinking sound, and she ducked down.

Casper rushed behind the car next to them, a red sedan, and disappeared. She moved through the pain as she tried to follow him. Two vehicles over, she still hadn't caught up with Casper, but she could see him through the window of the truck that was between them. Glancing in the truck's window, she spotted an aluminum baseball bat in the back seat.

"Casper," she whispered, trying to be just loud enough that only he could hear.

He turned and she pointed at the bat. A smile erupted on his face. On his side, the window was cracked just enough, and he slipped his arm inside and pulled the weapon out. She lifted the canister in her hands. Pain shot through her again, but as he nodded, his smile widened and it helped to control the ache in her side. All she had to do was concentrate on how to make it out of here and then she could think about the pain.

"Greg!" she yelled, pulling the pin from the fire extinguisher. "The only piece of garbage I ever allowed in my life was you."

Greg's evil laughter rang out through the garage—he sounded as though he was moving closer. "I'm glad you didn't try to argue your skills in the bedroom. I've had socks that were more adventurous than you."

Under normal circumstances, what the man was saying might have bothered her, but a condemnation coming from a mad man didn't really have the same amount of sting as if it had come from someone she actually cared about.

Casper twisted the bat in his hand, wringing it like he was envisioning it as Greg's neck.

Here, boy... she thought, wishing she could lure Greg closer like the dog he was. Though, a dog would have probably been more loyal. To call him one was a disservice to animals.

"If I was so bad in bed, why did you keep coming back for more?" She tried to laugh, but the sound was strained, and all she could really think about was her shaking hands. Hopefully, she could do what needed to be done.

"I'm not going to turn down free and easy."

She hated him. If she got the chance, killing him would be something she wouldn't regret. Casper moved toward the front of the truck, readying himself to pounce. It would be a race to see who could get to the jerk first.

"Is that what you told Michelle about me? Or did you even admit you were cheating on her, too?"

"She didn't need to know about you." Greg

was so close now that she could make out the sounds of his footfalls.

Just a few more feet.

Her hands were violently shaking.

"Had the stupid woman just not lost her nerve... That family can all go to hell." He was so close she could hear his labored breathing. There was the grinding of dirt under his shoes as he moved next to the car beside her.

She couldn't wait—any closer and he would have a shot at her.

He couldn't get a chance to raise his weapon.

After lifting the black hose over the top of the car, she hit the release and opened up the fire extinguisher. The white foam flew out in the direction of her attacker.

The diversion worked and she stood up and rushed toward the man, but Casper was already ahead of her. Watching in relief and shock, Casper drew back the baseball bat and swung with all of his power, striking Greg square in the side. Greg started to lift his arm and Casper struck him again, in the arm. Greg released the gun in his hand and it fell to the concrete floor.

Still pressing the trigger, she rushed toward the weapon, kicking it out and sending it skittering and under a car.

Greg fell to his knees, holding his arm and side. He was wailing in pain and anger, a string of expletives pouring from his mouth—none more colorful than what he was saying about her.

Casper moved to swing again, but she put up her hand, stopping him. "No more. The police can deal with him. They are on their way. He will be arrested."

"Don't you hear him? What he's saying about you?" Casper pointed at him, angry and full of rage.

"Yes, but you are better than he can ever hope to be. You are my future. He is my past. If you beat him to death, then we will have become the monsters."

Chapter Twenty-Six

She had known her future was bright, but Kristin had never expected to be flying the brand-new Madison County SAR, FLIR-equipped helo with Casper at her side. After months of waiting for the trial and sitting on the witness stand, Greg had been found guilty of murder in the first degree in the case of both Michelle and Hugh. He was still awaiting sentencing, but from what the prosecutor said, he would likely get life without the chance of parole.

Casper was on the phone with William, who had fully recovered and was spending some time in Maui in an effort to help him to move forward. He'd found a new girlfriend who'd agreed to go with him, and things seemed to be going well for him after his suicide attempt.

She smiled over at Casper and he made a silly, tongue-out face and she giggled. The action pulled at her scar from her bullet wound. It had taken longer than she would have liked to recover from being shot, but she had made use of every moment of downtime from work over the last eight months and had finally gotten her pilot's license. Really, it had all been thanks to Casper. Last month, she'd even transferred to his SAR team as a FLIR tech for their new bird—her bosses had been great in allowing her to work from home.

Everything was finally on the upswing and even things between her and Casper had been better than ever.

"You're doing great, babe," he said, hanging up the phone. He pointed toward a flat spot in a mountain meadow. "Why don't you put her down right there? I'm ready for lunch."

She dropped the bird, landing gently before powering down. "I can't believe you never told me how fun this was before."

"It is so freeing, flying," he said, smiling as he unclipped his belt and stepped down from the bird after the blades stopped spinning. "After everything we've been through, I'm proud of you." He grabbed his backpack.

She truly, deeply loved this man. Seeing him looking at her the way he was, with admiration, pride and familiarity, she found that the true freedom came with having him at her side.

Getting out, she followed Grover and him to the heart of the clearing and helped Casper spread out the blanket they had brought for their mountain picnic. Grover charged off into the distance, staying close enough to be seen, but far enough to sniff away.

In all of her dreams of the future, she had never imagined herself being a pilot, but after Greg's attack…she needed to become someone new, someone Greg hadn't known or damaged.

In spite of Greg and with the help of Casper, she had become even more independent and stronger than before.

Casper set out the food—a tray of meats, fruit and cheese and a bottle of red wine. In the middle of the tray was a little black box. Her heart moved into her throat. That box… It couldn't have been what she thought—or, rather *hoped*—it was.

"Casper?" She said his name like it was a question.

"Yes?" He sent her the knowing grin that she had come to love so much over the last few months.

"What is that? Some sort of dip?" she teased, pointing at the ring box.

"Oh, if you want it to be, but it was slightly more expensive than your traditional mustard." He dropped to one knee and picked up the box, then opened it.

Inside, tucked into the folds of velvet, was a simple gold band with inset channel diamonds.

She sucked in her breath, realizing how silly she must have sounded in teasing him, but realizing that this simple exchange, this *authenticity*, was who they were as a couple. They would never be perfect, they would say and do dumb things, but when it came down to what was important—each other—they would never give up.

"Kristin, I have loved you since the first moment I met you… In a moment of pain and sorrow, you lifted my grief and carried it until I could heal. Then I helped you in your time of healing. Together, we have been through so much, and as hard as it has been, and though we have already suffered, I wouldn't wish for anything but to spend my life with you."

She smiled widely, tears filling her eyes.

"Would you do me the honor of becoming my wife?"

Looking into his eyes, she saw only one thing—their future. It was incredibly bright.

"I know it's not mustard, but…" He paused, a faint blush rising in his cheeks that made her realize that he must have been thinking she was about to refuse.

"Oh, no."

"No?" he choked, sounding crestfallen.

"No, I mean *yes*. I will marry you." She put

her hands over her mouth as she skipped from one foot to the other in excitement. "I love you, Casper Keller. I want to be your Mrs. Keller, from this day and to the rest of time—with or without mustard."

He laughed and there was a look of relief on his face as he reached into the box and took out the ring. Gently, he slipped it onto her finger. "I love you, too, Mrs. Keller. You are my queen."

She leaned down and put her forehead to his, pulling his scent deeply into her lungs. "And you—you are my king."

"We will be side by side forever," he said, taking her hands in his.

She moved to kiss him. "Yes, my love, *forever.*"

* * * * *

*Look for more books in the
Big Sky Search and Rescue miniseries
by Danica Winters when* Swiftwater Enemies
goes on sale next month!